SUCCESS PRINCIPLES OF

JEFF BEZOS

SUCCESS PRINCIPLES OF
JEFF BEZOS

SHIKHA SHARMA

PRABHAT PRAKASHAN

Published by
PRABHAT PRAKASHAN PVT. LTD.
4/19 Asaf Ali Road,
New Delhi-110 002 (INDIA)
e-mail: prabhatbooks@gmail.com

ISBN 978-93-5562-398-0

SUCCESS PRINCIPLES OF JEFF BEZOS
by Shikha Sharma

Edition
First, 2024

Price
₹ 300 (Rupees Three Hundred Only)

Printed at
Sanjay Printers, Sahibabad

Author's Note

Jeff Bezos, the visionary founder of Amazon, has revolutionized the way we shop, read, and interact with technology. His remarkable journey from a small online bookstore to a global e-commerce giant platform has inspired entrepreneurs and business leaders worldwide. Through this book, I aim to dissect the principles and mindset that propelled Jeff Bezos to his incredible success.

As an avid follower of Jeff Bezos's career, I have always been fascinated by the unique qualities that define his approach to business and life. In the coming pages, I have meticulously explained the key principles that have contributed to his spectacular and rapid rise.

Success Principles of Jeff Bezos is a comprehensive exploration of the strategies and philosophies that have guided his decisions and actions. By delving into his mindset, decision-making processes, and leadership style, I hope to provide the readers with valuable insights and lessons that can be applied in the real business world.

Throughout this book, the readers will discover the importance of customer obsession, the relentless pursuit of innovation, and the willingness to embrace failure as a stepping stone to success. We will delve into the significance of long-term thinking, a core principle that has shaped Amazon's strategy and differentiation in the market. Additionally, we will explore the vital role of experimentation, data-driven decision-making, the power of building a strong organizational culture and so much more.

I have drawn from a wide range of resources, including interviews, articles, and Jeff Bezos's own writings and speeches, to present a comprehensive and authentic portrayal of his principles. However, it is important to note that this book is not an endorsement or reflection of Jeff Bezos's personal life or ethical choices. Rather, it focuses solely on his business strategies and success principles.

As the readers embark on this journey through the success principles of Jeff Bezos, I encourage them to reflect on how these principles can be adapted and applied to their own endeavours. May this book serve as a source of inspiration, guidance, and practical advice to the readers as they pursue their own paths to success.

❑

Contents

Be Obsessed with Creating Value

The best way to become successful in life is by adding value to the lives of the people around you. The more you help others, the more you will achieve. What you give to the universe will ultimately be returned to you. Therefore, by helping others you are helping yourself.

Likewise, Bezos firmly believes that creating value for customers is the foundation of a thriving business. For any business to flourish, value creation is essential because that is what sets you apart from all your competitors. If your product is unable to create significant value in the life of the customer, then it will be seen as just another product in the market, having no exceptional quality that differentiates it from others. Thus, your product needs to be a unique offering to the customers'.

Understanding the importance of creating value, Bezos makes all his decisions from his customer's perspective. In a letter to Amazon's shareholders, Bezos requested his team to create more than they consume to become successful in business. In his letter, he wrote, "If you want to be successful in business, you must create more than you consume. Your goal should be to create value for everyone you interact with. Any business that does not create value for those it touches, even if it appears successful on the surface, will not last long in this world. It is on the way out."

In Bezos's view, being obsessed with creating value requires a deep understanding of customers' evolving preferences and a commitment to exceed their expectations. He emphasizes the need for companies to listen to their customers, gather their feedback, and use the gathered data to drive continuous improvement. By incorporating customer feedback into the development process, businesses can tailor their offerings to meet specific needs of their customers, ensuring an ongoing cycle of value creation.

Bezos also encourages entrepreneurs to think of long-term gains rather than being fixated on short-term gains if they want to create value for their customers. According to him, sustained success comes from consistently delivering value over time. Moreover, it is important to note that Bezos's focus on creating value extends beyond customer satisfaction. In fact, he believes in creating value for all stakeholders, including employees, partners, and shareholders.

Therefore, to become the earth's most customer-centric company, Bezos is obsessed with adding value to everyone's life. As the renowned author, Robin Sharma has once said, "Money is a function of creating value. The more value you create for other people, the higher the sales of your organization."

Thus, to become indispensable to people, you must go beyond their expectations and show them that you care about them by prioritizing and understanding their needs.

Lesson: *The key to success in life is by adding value to the lives of others. By helping others, you also help yourself.*

❑

Don't Sweat for Small Stuff, Hire Experts for It

In an organization, there are many things that need to be taken care of. Many decisions need to be made from 'which tea to be served in the canteen' to 'which marketing strategy need to be used for promoting a certain product.' As a single person cannot make all these decisions alone, the need of a delegation becomes important.

As a clever businessman, Bezos follows the policy of 'not to sweat about the small stuff.' He understands that he alone cannot handle the whole business and he needs to delegate his work to experts to run a successful operation. Hence, he believes in delegating his tasks and hiring experts to handle the intricacies and minutiae of day-to-day operations. This is why, in the context of small decisions, Bezos says, "These decisions can and should be made quickly by high judgement individuals or small groups."

According to Bezos, as a leader, it is crucial to prioritize and invest your time and energy wisely. Instead of getting caught up in every small detail or trying to micromanage every aspect of the business, he advocates for delegating tasks to competent professionals. Bezos believes that building a team of experts who excel in their respective areas, allows one to concentrate on higher-level responsibilities. Moreover, having a team of smart professionals makes one's job easy and hassle-free, as now one need not tell them how to do their job.

By hiring experts, Bezos ensures that the best individuals are tackling the specific challenges that they are qualified for. He understands that professionals with specialized skills and knowledge are more equipped to handle complex tasks efficiently and effectively rather than an individual who lacks adequate knowledge. This allows him to focus on the broader vision, strategic planning, and critical decision-making that helps propel the company forward.

Moreover, delegation of work allows the decisions to be made efficiently and quickly. This in turn, saves the valuable time and energy of individuals as they focus only on a specific task. Delegation of work also helps the individuals to achieve meaningful results as they focus on one task at a time.

Lastly, Bezos reminds us that it is important to note that not sweating about the small stuff does not mean ignoring details altogether. In fact, it is a good habit to pay attention to details, especially when it comes to customer experience and product quality. However, delegating operational tasks, administrative duties, and other small-scale responsibilities to capable professionals make it possible for individuals to saves their time and mental energy for more strategic endeavours. Thus, hire smart and wise professionals to do your work so that you do not have to sweat about every single detail.

Lesson: *Delegating work allows decisions to be made quickly and saves valuable time and energy.*

❑

Don't Stall on Making Decisions

In today's fast-paced and competitive world, opportunities arise and evolve rapidly. By stalling on making decisions, we risk losing out on favourable circumstances or being overtaken by more agile competitors. Prompt decision-making allows us to seize opportunities and stay ahead in both the game of life and business.

According to Bezos, as time waits for no one, we must make swift and smart decisions. He often says that "you have worn me down" is an awful decision-making process. It is slow and de-energizing. So, go for quick escalation instead—it is better. Not only would it increase your productivity level and save you time but it would also help you overcome procrastination. In addition, Bezos believes that waiting for perfect information or absolute certainty can lead to missed opportunities. Instead, he advocates for using available data and insights to make informed decisions promptly. Therefore, making quick decisions is crucial because opportunities do not come knocking on your door every day.

Likewise, Bezos encourages individuals to make high-quality decisions at a high velocity. According to him, quick decision-making prompts us to take action on our ideas instead of hesitating and overestimating the risk count. He understands that not all decisions will be correct, but the key is to learn from failures and iterate quickly. Moreover, by making decisions promptly, entrepreneurs can gather feedback and adjust their strategies in a timely manner, enabling faster progress and innovation.

Furthermore, Bezos recognizes the importance of avoiding analysis paralysis. According to him, excessively dwelling on decision-making can lead to indecisiveness and wasted time. Bezos encourages leaders to strike a balance between gathering necessary information and taking action. He advocates for using a combination of data-driven insights, intuition, and experience to make informed decisions efficiently.

Additionally, the idea of a "two-way door" decision is often emphasized by Bezos. He believes that most of the decisions can be reversible or customizable, considering they need modification. Because of their ability to adapt and pivot, if their initial choice proves to be ineffective, leaders can make such decisions without having an excessive amount of anxiety about failing. On the contrary, there are some decisions that need to make only after prolonged contemplation because failing or delay of these decisions can cause irreversible damage. Such decisions should be made only after considering all parameters.

To make a long story short, time is a valuable asset which should not be wasted by prolonged deliberation. When decisions are made promptly, it streamlines processes, eliminates unnecessary delays, and ensures that resources are allocated effectively. It allows individuals and teams to focus their efforts on implementation and achieving desired outcomes. Remember as Bezos often says, “Speed matters in business - plus a high-velocity decision-making environment is more fun too.” Therefore, do not stall on decision-making. Instead make high-velocity decisions to prevent unnecessary dwelling.

Lesson: *Prompt decision-making is crucial in today’s fast-paced and competitive world. By hesitating, we risk losing out on opportunities.*

❑

Sell the Solution to a Need

A customer does not care about you or your product. It does not matter to him/her how great your product is or how much time and energy you have spent creating it because a customer's only concern is finding a solution to his/her problem.

Customers spend their hard-earned money on products and services that resolve their problems and fulfil their needs. Hence, a business is not about selling products but selling solutions to a customer's problems. Jeff Bezos has emphasized the importance of selling a solution to a need rather than just a product because he understands that successful businesses are built on understanding and addressing the needs of their customers. By focusing on providing solutions that meet those needs, companies can create long-lasting customer relationships and drive sustained growth.

When Bezos decided to start his own company, he realized that entrepreneurs do not make money when they sell things, rather they make money when they help their customers make better purchasing decisions. According to him, making money is all about making people's lives easier and hassle-free. This is why, Amazon aims to become the earth's most customer-centric company.

According to Bezos, the key to effective selling lies in identifying and understanding the underlying needs and desires of customers. Rather than simply promoting a product's features or attributes, Bezos advocates for emphasizing how a product or service solves a problem or fulfils a customer's specific need. By aligning offerings with the customer's pain points or aspirations, businesses can create a compelling value proposition that resonates with their target audience. As Bezos once said, "We do not make money by selling things. We make money by helping our customers make better purchasing decisions."

This is why, Bezos suggests that the solution-selling method is more effective instead of the traditional sales process. Because rather than pushing your product on your customer, it focuses on providing the best possible solution to a customer's particular problem. It is a practical and empathetic process which allows us to understand things from the customer's perspective.

After all, making money is no longer about selling your products or services but making people's life easier. It is important to note that Bezos's perspective extends beyond immediate sales transactions. He advocates to provide exceptional solutions and exceptional customer experiences so that companies could foster customer loyalty, repeat business, and positive word-of-mouth referrals. Thus, leading to a sustainable growth in business.

Therefore, instead of trying to sell a product or service, approach each customer with the intention of assisting them in achieving a goal or solving a problem.

Lesson: *Effective selling involves identifying and understanding customer desires and aligning offerings with their pain points.*

❑

Put Customers at the Centre of Your Universe

For a business to flourish, the companies must clearly understand their customers' needs. You will never become a customer-centric company without having a clear insight of your customers' needs. Hence, companies need to adopt their customers' perspectives. Bezos firmly believes that customer satisfaction is paramount to business success and growth. By prioritizing the needs and experiences of customers, companies can build strong relationships, drive innovation, and thrive in competitive markets.

Bezos attributes Amazon's success to their customer-centric strategies. He says, "There are many ways to centre a business. You can be competitor-focused, product-focused, technology-focused or business model-focused. But in my view, being customer obsessive is by far more productive." It is because according to him customers are always dissatisfied. He proclaims that "even when the customers report being happy and the business is going well, they are still wonderfully dissatisfied. Without their knowledge, customers always want something better."

As Bezos puts his customers at the centre of his universe, his every action and decision synchronize with this belief. For instance, with the launch of Amazon Prime membership, Jeff was enabled to enhance customer experience. Results showed that the Prime customers found the concept of free and one-day shipping extraordinary. Thus, they end up spending significantly higher than non-Prime customers.

Another example of his customer obsessive mindset is the introduction of customer reviews. As Bezos wanted to go beyond his limit to help his customers, he encouraged his customers to provide feedback on the product range to help the prospective buyers. Thus, Bezos always says, "We see our customers as guests to a party and we are the host. It is our job to make every important aspect of the customer experience a bit better, every day."

Moreover, Bezos believes in building trust and loyalty by consistently delivering exceptional value. This involves going above and beyond to meet customer expectations, providing excellent customer service, and resolving issues promptly and efficiently. By prioritizing customer satisfaction, companies can foster a positive reputation, generate repeat business, and benefit from positive word-of-mouth referrals.

Bezos also emphasizes the significance of customer-driven innovation. He encourages companies to obsess over comprehending and anticipating customer needs before they are fully articulated. Companies can maintain a competitive edge and drive continuous improvement by anticipating customer needs and actively developing solutions to meet them.

Hence, it is essential for businesses to put the customer at the centre of their universe because it helps to create meaningful and long-lasting relationships with customers. Thus, leading the companies towards success.

Lesson: *Customer satisfaction is paramount to success. To flourish, businesses must understand customer needs.*

❑

Be Terrified of Your Customers

In one of his annual newsletters to stakeholders, Bezos explained how he always reminds his employees to wake up terrified of their customers. He believes a business becomes what it is because of its customers. Therefore, we must keep pace with our customers' interests and requirements.

In the newsletter Bezos wrote, "Yes, you should wake every morning terrified with your sheets drenched in sweat, but not because you are afraid of competitors. Be afraid of customers, because those are the people who have the money. Our competitors are never going to send us money."

Therefore, if your business is competitor-focused, soon your business will lose its distinction. By the end, the only difference between you and your competitors will be the price range and brand name. For instance, let's take the example of fast-food franchises like Pizza Hut, Domino's Pizza and Papa John's

Pizza. They all provide almost similar services and there is not much distinction between them.

It is understandable to be wary of your competition but if you focus on your customers' interests and preferences then the chances of your success will be greater. As Bezos says, "We keep our competitors focused on us, while we stay focused on the customer."

Remember your customers stay loyal to you till they find someone with a better offer. Therefore, Bezos reminds you to be afraid of your customers. With their choices, they could either make you or break you. Every day you must upgrade yourself and your product to meet the expectations of your customers; otherwise, you will be out of the business soon.

Bezos believes that complacency is the kiss of death. Therefore, for every organization it is crucial to maintain a sense of wariness or caution against customers. Moreover, fear works well as a motivator for companies to commit to constant improvement, experimentation and innovation.

According to Bezos, fear helps drive a hard working attitude and inventive reasoning in the employees. It is our customers who create the foundation of every business's growth. In this highly competitive world, if the companies will not constantly try to provide better results, then there will be only one way for them to go, i.e. down.

In an interview, recalling his past, Bezos mentioned how Amazon first started as a small company that used to sell only books online. Thanks to Bezos and his team's relentless efforts that Amazon transformed into the world's leading online retailer. Today, Amazon sells everything from entertainment and healthcare to electronic gadgets.

This is why, Bezos credits his and Amazon's success to his obsession to become the most customer-centric company.

He recognized early that to become successful and be able to meet his customers' requirements, he must consider customers' perspectives in every decision that he and his company made. Hence, Bezos encourages businesses to develop a healthy sense of wariness against customers so that they will always be motivated to work hard towards innovation.

Lesson: *Complacency leads to failure, fear serves as a motivator for improvement and innovation.*

❑

The Empty Chair Principle

The "Empty Chair Principle" is a management technique or practice proposed by Jeff Bezos that involves leaving an empty chair in a meeting or discussion to represent the absent or hypothetical customer or stakeholder. This principle signifies the presence of the customer's voice and perspective in important decision-making discussions and meetings, even when the customer is not physically present.

According to the "Empty Chair Principle," an empty chair symbolizes the presence of the customer, and it serves as a constant reminder to consider the customer's point of view and interests in all business discussions and decision-making processes. The presence of an empty chair serves as a reminder that the customer's needs, preferences, and satisfaction should always be at the forefront of the organization's priorities. Basically, every action of a company in some way or other must improve the lives of its customers.

Bezos recognizes that the "Empty Chair Principle" offers several benefits for businesses. Firstly, it serves as a constant reminder to prioritize the customer's viewpoint and interests. It helps to prevent discussions from becoming solely focused on internal agendas, biases, or assumptions. By including the customer's perspective, businesses can make more informed decisions that better align with customer needs and preferences.

Secondly, the "Empty Chair Principle" encourages empathy and fosters a deeper understanding of the customer experience. Participants are prompted to consider how decisions may impact customers and to think from their perspective. This empathetic approach can lead to improved products, services, and overall customer satisfaction.

Bezos also believes that by adopting the "Empty Chair Principle," businesses can enhance their problem-solving capabilities. Participants are encouraged to think creatively and critically, exploring innovative solutions that address customer pain points or challenges. This approach can lead to more effective problem-solving and the development of solutions that resonate with the intended audience.

Moreover, Bezos advocates that considering the customer's perspective through the "Empty Chair Principle" enables businesses to anticipate and proactively address future customer needs. By evaluating decisions from the standpoint of potential customers, organizations can stay ahead of the curve and adapt to changing market dynamics more effectively.

When asked about the reason behind his and Amazon's success, Bezos always said, "The no.1 thing that has made us successful by far is our obsessive-compulsive focus on the customer." Through his actions, interviews and speeches, Bezos has consistently reminded the world that the most important person for every business is the customer.

Ultimately, the "Empty Chair Principle" reflects Bezos customer-focused philosophy and the emphasis he places on building a customer-centric culture within organizations. By keeping the customer's perspective at the forefront, businesses can make decisions that better align with customer needs, drive customer loyalty, and deliver exceptional experiences. Hence, the principle serves as a symbolic reminder to prioritize the customer's voice and perspective in all decision-making discussions.

Lesson: *Prioritizing the customer's viewpoint and interests helps prevent internally-focused discussions and biases by including the customer's perspective in decision-making.*

❑

Type 1 and Type 2 Decisions

To become a successful business magnate, Bezos follows the methodology of Type 1 and Type 2 decisions. According to him, decisions could be classified into two categories based on their reversible nature.

In Bezos's opinion, Type 1 decisions are characterized as irreversible or high-impact choices that require thoughtful consideration and analysis. These decisions often involve significant resources, long-term implications, and have a lasting and enduring impact on the direction of the business. Bezos emphasizes the need to be deliberate and meticulous in making Type 1 decisions, as they set the foundation for the company's future.

Bezos believes that Type 1 decisions typically involve strategic initiatives, technological investments, major acquisitions, or large-scale infrastructure projects. These choices are made after conducting extensive research, gathering data, and engaging in thorough analysis. Bezos encourages a data-driven approach to

Type 1 decisions by leveraging metrics, market insights, and customer feedback to inform the decision-making process.

It is crucial to be willing to accept accountability for Type 1 decisions, as they carry significant weight and can shape the trajectory of the organization. Bezos emphasizes the importance of avoiding unnecessary reversals or changes in Type 1 decisions, as doing so may lead to wasted resources and missed opportunities.

On the other hand, Bezos describes Type 2 decisions as reversible or low-impact choices that can be easily adjusted or course-corrected. These decisions are more experimental and iterative in nature, allowing for learning and adaptation along the way. Bezos encourages a culture of embracing failure and learning from mistakes in Type 2 decisions.

Type 2 decisions often involve operational processes, product features, marketing campaigns, or other areas where experimentation and rapid iteration are possible. Bezos believes in empowering employees to make Type 2 decisions independently, promoting a decentralized decision-making environment that fosters innovation and agility.

Tragically, often it is not difficult to confuse a Type 2 decision for a Type 1 decision or allow wariness to sneak in and expect that each Type 2 decision is a Type 1 decision. Doing this will make you paralyzed and you will end up making no decision at all.

In an annual stakeholder newsletter, Bezos wrote, "Some decisions are consequential and irreversible or nearly irreversible—one-way doors—and these decisions must be made methodically, carefully, slowly, with great deliberation and consultation. If you walk through and do not like what you see on the other side, you cannot get back to where you were before. We can call these Type 1 decisions. But most decisions are not like that—they are changeable, reversible—they are two-way doors.

If you have made a sub-optimal Type 2 decision, you do not have to live with the consequences for that long. You can reopen the door and go back through. Type 2 decisions can and should be made quickly by high judgement individuals or small groups." He further continues, "As organizations get larger, there seems to be a tendency to use the heavyweight Type 1 decision-making process on most decisions, including many Type 2 decisions. The end result of this is slowness, unthoughtful risk aversion, failure to experiment sufficiently, and consequently diminished invention."

Therefore, using the Type 1 and Type 2 decision methodology brings strategic clarity, optimizes resource allocation, manages risk, fosters innovation, and enhances adaptability. By understanding the nature of decisions and aligning them with the organization's strategic goals, businesses can make informed choices that balance long-term vision with swift execution. Hence, this methodology promotes a structured approach to decision-making and contributes to organizational success in dynamic and competitive environments.

Lesson: *Decisions are irreversible choices with long-term impact on the business, such as strategic initiatives or major acquisitions.*

❑

Be the First to Begin

Being the first to begin implies being at the forefront of change, whether it is entering a new market, introducing a unique product or service, or adopting a disruptive approach. It requires vision, courage, and a willingness to take calculated risks. By being the first mover, individuals or businesses can shape industries, set trends, and establish themselves as leaders or influencers in their respective fields.

As a result, Bezos has often advocated to being the first to begin in the realm of entrepreneurship and innovation. He believes that taking the initiative and being the first to enter a market or pursue a new idea can provide significant advantages for businesses.

According to Bezos, being the first to begin allows businesses to establish themselves as pioneers and gain a head start over competitors. By entering a market early, businesses can capture market share, build brand recognition, and shape the industry's direction. This first-mover advantage can provide a strong foundation for long-term success.

Known for his relentless pursuit of innovation and disruption, Bezos has demonstrated a willingness to enter new markets, challenge established norms, and pioneer new initiatives throughout his career. By being the first to begin, Bezos and Amazon have been able to carve out new opportunities and gain competitive advantages over the years.

For instance, take the example of Amazon's early entry into the e-commerce industry. When Bezos founded Amazon in 1994, the concept of online shopping was relatively new. By being the first to seize the potential of e-commerce and establish a robust online marketplace, Amazon was able to revolutionize retail and transformed the way people shop.

Bezos recognizes that being the first to begin enables businesses to learn and iterate faster. By entering a market early, entrepreneurs can gather valuable insights, learn from initial successes and failures, and refine their strategies and offerings. This rapid learning process allows businesses to adapt and improve their products or services more quickly, enhancing their competitive edge.

Moreover, Bezos believes that being a pioneer in a specific field or industry can establish credibility and authority. By taking the lead and demonstrating expertise, individuals or organizations can become influencers, shaping industry standards, and driving conversations.

In addition, being the first to begin enables access to early feedback from customers or users. This feedback loop facilitates continuous improvement and refinement of products or services, ensuring that subsequent iterations better align with customer needs and preferences.

However, Bezos understands that being the first to begin does not guarantee success on its own. He emphasizes the importance of execution, customer focus, and continuous improvement. Merely being the first in a market or pursuing a new idea is not enough; businesses must also deliver exceptional products, provide outstanding customer experiences, and continually innovate to maintain their competitive advantage.

Therefore, it is essential to note that when you start the business of your dreams earlier, you have more time to develop your skills, learn from your mistakes, build relationships, and gain a competitive advantage. It makes way for long-haul achievement and positions early starters as pioneers and trailblazers in their businesses.

Lesson: *Establish yourself as pioneer and gain a head start over competitors.*

❑

Regret Minimization Framework

At the age of 30, Jeff Bezos came up with a brilliant but risky idea. The idea was to quit his well-established career and start an online book store in his garage. He shared his decision with his wife and boss. His wife was supported the idea, his boss on the other hand, told him to think it over for 48 hours before finalizing his decision. After pondering for the said time, Bezos decided to go ahead with his idea and he ended up quitting his job. On this decision he commented, "Though it was a difficult decision to make, he didn't regret it."

Recognizing the importance of minimizing regrets in life and decision-making, Bezos came up with a unique mental model that allows him to take action more swiftly on ideas that he had been brooding over for some time. He called this framework "Regret Minimization Framework."

In an interview, Bezos explained why he came up with this mental model. He said that the idea of this framework is to imagine yourself in the future and evaluate your choice from that point of view. For every new idea, Bezos thought to himself that when he would be 80 years old, would he regret not trying that particular idea? His answer then would determine his decision.

According to Bezos, adopting a long-term perspective when making decisions allows room to minimize the chances of future regrets. He stresses the importance of considering the potential consequences and implications of choices, both in the short and long-term. By carefully weighing options and evaluating the potential outcomes, individuals can make more informed decisions and minimize the likelihood of regret.

The "Regret Minimization Framework" also aligns with Bezos's philosophy of embracing bold, innovative ideas and taking calculated risks. He advocates to individuals to prioritize personal growth, learning, and seizing opportunities to avoid the regret of inaction or missed possibilities.

Furthermore, Bezos believes that minimizing regrets also involves embracing a mindset of experimentation and embracing failure as a learning opportunity. He understands that avoiding risks altogether may lead to regrets of missed opportunities. He believes that setbacks and mistakes are valuable learning experiences that can help make informed future decisions and lead to personal growth. By embracing failure as a natural part of the journey, individuals can minimize regrets by viewing setbacks as opportunities for improvement.

Moreover, Bezos points out that when regrets are minimized, individuals can feel a sense of fulfilment and contentment with their life choices. It also reduces the burden of dwelling on past decisions and allows for a more positive and forward-looking mindset. Thus, providing an opportunity to become more self-resilient and successful.

In addition, Bezos encourages individuals to follow their instincts and make choices aligned with their values and aspirations. He believes that while gathering information is important, it is also crucial to trust your instincts and intuition. Your intuition often provides valuable insights that logical analysis may not capture. Honouring your gut feelings can help you make choices that align with your deeper sense of purpose and minimize future regrets.

Frequently, Bezos has mentioned how all his best decisions in business and in life have been made with heart, intuition, guts—not analysis. He further points out that "there has to be risk taking. You have to have instinct. All the good decisions have to be made that way."

However, Bezos also recognizes that developing a resilient attitude is crucial to bounce back from setbacks and adapt to unexpected outcomes. Resilience enables you to navigate challenges with a positive mindset and view them as learning experiences rather than sources of regret. Thus, reducing the rate of regrets in one's life.

At the end, it is crucial to note that by making informed decisions, learning from experiences, and staying true to personal values and aspirations, individuals can minimize the likelihood of future regrets and lead a more fulfilling and purposeful life.

Lesson: *By following instincts, embracing resilience, and staying true to personal values, individuals can lead a fulfilling and purposeful life with fewer regrets.*

❑

Be Different and Unique

Being different and unique means that you possess some qualities, characteristics, or perspectives that distinguish you from others. It involves embracing and expressing your individuality, standing out from the crowd, and offering something distinct that sets you apart.

Owing to his intelligence, Jeff Bezos recognizes the importance of being distinctive in order to stand out in a crowded marketplace. He understands that in today's competitive landscape, being different and unique is essential for success. He believes that copying or imitating others may lead to mediocrity, while embracing one's uniqueness can unlock opportunities for innovation and create a distinct competitive advantage.

According to Bezos, being different involves thinking independently and challenging the status quo. He encourages individuals and organizations to question existing norms, explore unconventional ideas, and not be afraid to take risks. By embracing their unique perspectives and pushing boundaries, individuals can discover new paths and opportunities that set them apart from the competition.

In one of his annual letters to stakeholders, Bezos wrote, "We all know that distinctiveness and originality are valuable. We are all taught to 'be yourself.' What I am really asking you to do is to embrace your uniqueness and be realistic about how much energy it takes to maintain that distinctiveness. The world wants you to be typical - in a thousand ways, it pulls at you. Don't let it happen."

He adds, "Differentiation is survival and the universe wants you to be typical. You have to pay a price for your distinctiveness, and it is worth it. The fairy tale version of 'be yourself' is that all the pain stops as soon as you allow your distinctiveness to shine. That version is misleading. Being yourself is worth it, but do not expect it to be easy or free. You will have to put energy into it continuously."

According to Bezos, there are many ways with which you can set yourself apart from your competitors. For instance, customer-centricity helps a business to develop distinction. By listening to customers, observing their behaviour, and going above and beyond to meet their expectations, individuals can create unique value propositions that resonate with their target audience. Thus, making them stand out among the crowd and maintain their distinctiveness.

Likewise, Bezos also encourages individuals to foster a culture of innovation and experimentation. He believes that by encouraging diverse perspectives, empowering employees to think creatively, and providing the necessary resources, organizations can cultivate an environment that breeds uniqueness. By embracing innovation, individuals can develop unique solutions, disrupt industries, and create a lasting impact.

Additionally, Bezos recognizes the value of embracing failure as a stepping stone to success by becoming a unique offering to the customers. He understands that taking risks and pursuing unique ideas may involve setbacks and failures along the way. However, he encourages individuals to learn from failures, iterate on approaches, and maintain a resilient attitude. By embracing failure as a learning opportunity, individuals can refine their uniqueness and drive future success.

All told, Bezos reinforces the importance of the idea of differentiation and embracing one's uniqueness. By thinking independently and challenging norms individuals can set themselves apart, create unique value, and thrive in competitive environments. Thus, one should embrace their uniqueness because that is what makes you great.

Lesson: *Being unique means having qualities or perspectives that distinguish you from others.*

❑

Work Like it is Day 1

"Work like it is Day 1" is a philosophy of Jeff Bezos that summarizes his idea of maintaining a startup mindset even as a company grows and evolves. He believes that approaching each day with the enthusiasm, creativity, and agility typically associated with the early stages of a business is essential for fostering innovation, staying nimble, and continually striving for excellence.

According to Bezos, "Day 1" signifies a state of constant alertness, customer-centricity, and a relentless focus on experimentation and invention. It embodies the spirit of taking risks, challenging the status quo, and consistently pushing the boundaries of what is achievable within a company. This approach is in stark contrast to a "Day 2" mindset, which Bezos describes as a state of complacency, risk aversion, and stagnation, often associated with established companies that have lost their drive for innovation and customer-centricity.

Often, Bezos was asked how does "Day 2" look like? In answer, he always says that "Day 2 is stasis. Followed by irrelevance. Followed by excruciating, painful decline. Followed by death. And that is why it is always Day 1 for Amazon."

Bezos firmly believes that the "Day 1" mentality involves several key aspects. Firstly, it entails maintaining a sense of urgency and avoiding complacency. Bezos understands that a sense of urgency can drive individuals and organizations to constantly challenge themselves, stay ahead of the competition, and seek opportunities for growth and improvement.

Secondly, Bezos emphasizes the importance of embracing a beginner's mindset. He encourages individuals to approach their work with curiosity, openness to new ideas, and a willingness to learn. By maintaining a humble and inquisitive attitude, individuals can continuously adapt, evolve, and avoid falling into the trap of relying on past successes.

Furthermore, Bezos promotes a culture of innovation and experimentation. He believes that embracing a "Day 1" mindset involves taking calculated risks, exploring new possibilities, and being willing to fail in the pursuit of breakthroughs. By fostering an environment that encourages experimentation, individuals can drive innovation, discover new avenues of growth, and continuously delight customers.

Moreover, Bezos recognizes that a "Day 1" mindset involves prioritizing sustainable growth over short-term gains. By maintaining a long-term perspective, individuals can make strategic decisions that contribute to the enduring success and impact of their endeavours.

Additionally, Bezos believes that a "Day 1" mentality requires an unwavering commitment to understanding and meeting customer needs. By listening to customers, obsessing over their satisfaction, and continuously raising the bar on delivering value, individuals can drive customer loyalty and maintain a competitive edge.

All told, "Day 1" approach has contributed to Bezos's and Amazon's sustainable success. The commitment to maintaining a startup mentality has not only driven Amazon's success but has also shaped the broader e-commerce and technology industries, inspiring countless companies to prioritize innovation, customer satisfaction, and a culture of continuous learning and improvement. Therefore, always work as if it is "Day 1" of your business or work if you want to grow consistently.

Lesson: *Have startup mindset even as a company grows and mindset of complacency and risk aversion.*

❑

Be Alert About Your Passion

Jeff Bezos, founder of Amazon and Blue Origin, has always believed that our passions choose us rather than us choosing our passions. The reason behind this belief is that he understands that a genuine passion arises from a deep-seated connection to a particular field or area of interest. He advocates the idea that true passion emerges naturally, often driven by an individual's intrinsic inclinations, curiosities, and unique life experiences. According to him, recognizing and acknowledging these innate passions can lead to a more fulfilling and purpose-driven life.

Often, Bezos is found quoting that "one of the huge mistakes people make is that they try to force an interest on themselves. You do not choose your passions; your passions choose you." The sentiment behind this statement is Bezos's belief that identifying and pursuing one's passion is crucial for personal fulfilment and success. He understands that when individuals are genuinely passionate about their work or pursuits, they are more likely to invest the necessary time, effort, and dedication to excel in their endeavours.

In Bezos's opinion, being alert to one's passion involves self-reflection and introspection. This is why, he encourages individuals to explore their interests, values, and aspirations to gain a deeper understanding of what truly drives them. By being attentive to their inner desires and inclinations, individuals can identify areas where their passion lies.

An example from Bezos's life that illustrates the significance of being attuned to one's passions is his unwavering commitment to technological innovation and his deep fascination with the possibilities of the internet. From the inception of Amazon, Bezos demonstrated a profound passion for leveraging technology to transform the way people shop and access information.

Likewise, Bezos's passion for space exploration has led him to found Blue Origin, a private aerospace manufacturer and spaceflight services company. Through Blue Origin, Bezos has continued to channel his passion for advancing space technology and exploration, demonstrating the importance of aligning personal passions with professional pursuits.

Now, Bezos understands the importance of aligning one's passion with their chosen field or career. He believes that when individuals are engaged in work that aligns with their passion, they are more likely to derive satisfaction, overcome challenges, and achieve remarkable outcomes. By pursuing opportunities that resonate with their passion, individuals can find greater fulfilment and make meaningful contributions.

Additionally, Bezos also asserts the need for perseverance and determination in pursuing one's passion. He understands that the path to success may not always be smooth, and individuals may encounter obstacles along the way. Thus, by remaining alert to their passion, individuals can stay motivated, persist through challenges, and continue to pursue their goals with enthusiasm and tenacity.

As a result, Bezos encourages individuals to constantly evaluate and reassess their passion as they grow and evolve. For he believes that passions may change or evolve over time, and it is important to stay attuned to these shifts. By being open to exploring new interests and possibilities, individuals can discover new passions or adapt their existing passions to new contexts. Therefore, always remember that discovering your passion is not just about career and money. Instead, it is about finding the real you, the one which has been hidden under the expectations of the world. So, free your true self and find what inspires you the most.

Lesson: *Passions choose us rather than the other way around, and recognizing and pursuing these innate passions can lead to a more fulfilling life.*

❑

Optimism is Must

Jeff Bezos's unwavering optimism has played a pivotal and key role in his entrepreneurial journey. Despite facing numerous challenges and setbacks in life, Bezos's optimism remained as a driving force that propelled him to sustainable success.

Time and again, Bezos's optimism has helped him to walk on the uncharted paths which often, if not always, has led him to success. For instance, Bezos was just 30 years old when he decided to quit his well-paid job to sell books online. In a time, when internet was not everyone's cup of tea, he decided to take his chance with internet. Looking at today, we could all say that he had made the best decision of his life years ago. But yet, if you have asked someone three decades ago, "Is internet worth you your time?" I am sure they would have told you "no." But now, we cannot even imagine our life without it.

Another example that illustrates the significance of optimism in Bezos's life is Kindle. When Bezos decided to launch Kindle, he was met with scepticism from the publishing industry. Despite this, he remained optimistic about the potential of e-readers. At the end, Bezos decided to advance with the development and launch of the Kindle, which ultimately helped to revolutionize the way people read and transformed the publishing industry.

This is why, Bezos believes that optimism is a crucial attribute for individuals and organizations to navigate through difficult times and pursue ambitious goals. He understands that maintaining a positive outlook can fuel motivation, resilience, and a willingness to take risks.

From Bezos's perspective, optimism involves having a belief in the potential for positive outcomes, even in the face of setbacks or obstacles. He encourages individuals to approach challenges with a mindset that embraces possibilities and seeks solutions. For he believes that by maintaining optimism, individuals can overcome adversity, find creative solutions, and make progress towards their goals.

Furthermore, Bezos believes that setbacks and challenges encountered along the way are often temporary and can serve learning opportunities. Hence, by focusing on the bigger picture and maintaining a belief in the future, individuals can maintain a sense of optimism and persevere through difficult times.

Bezos also recognizes that the power of optimism could be used to inspire and motivate teams. He believes that if leaders communicate a positive vision to their teams, then they could instil a sense of purpose within them and inspire them to believe in the possibilities ahead. Thus, by cultivating an optimistic work environment, leaders can foster a culture of innovation, collaboration, and growth.

Likewise, Bezos understands that optimism helps individuals to embrace a learning and open mindset. He believes that maintaining a curious and open mindset, coupled with optimism, enables individuals to adapt, innovate, and seize new opportunities. Therefore, by embracing change and seeing it as a chance for growth, individuals can approach challenges with optimism and find ways to turn them into advantages.

Ultimately, Bezos's philosophy highlights the power of maintaining an optimistic outlook in fostering growth, innovation, and progress. Though optimism is one of the key principles that lead individuals to the path of success, it is also important to note that it needs to be balanced with a sense of realism. Remember not to get carried away solely with positive expectations but approach situations with a clear understanding of the challenges and risks involved. As Bezos says, "Though we are optimistic, we must remain vigilant and maintain a sense of urgency."

Lesson: *Optimism can inspire and motivate teams, foster a culture of innovation and collaboration, and help individuals embrace a learning and open mindset that leads to growth and success.*

❑

Have Fun Along the Way

In the fast-paced world of business and entrepreneurship, the pursuit of success often overshadows the simple joy of the journey. However, Jeff Bezos, the visionary founder of Amazon, has continually stressed the importance of finding enjoyment and fulfilment in the process of achieving one's goals. Bezos is known not just for his determination and innovative ideas but also for his support for adding enjoyment to the path of achieving success.

According to Bezos, the concept of "having fun along the way" is not just about adding fun to work; rather, it encompasses a holistic approach to life and work that fosters creativity, motivation, and overall well-being. Throughout his career, Bezos has led by example, incorporating this principle into various aspects of his professional life.

One of the most striking illustrations of Bezos's commitment to this philosophy can be found within the work culture at Amazon itself. By cultivating a work environment that encourages a healthy balance between hard work and enjoyment, Bezos has fostered a culture where employees are inspired to think creatively and passionately about their roles. This approach has resulted in groundbreaking innovations such as Amazon Prime and the development of Amazon Web Services, both of which have redefined their respective industries.

Apart from Amazon, Bezos has also ventured into other fields that has sparked his curiosity and passion. He has an aerospace company called Blue Origin which serves as a testament to his fascination with space exploration. Moreover, his unwavering enthusiasm for this venture has not only demonstrated his dedication to pushing the boundaries of science and technology but also highlights his ability to find joy in exploring the unknown.

Bezos's diverse range of interests also extends to his ownership of *The Washington Post*, his involvement in Amazon Studios, and his establishment of the Bezos Earth Fund. These ventures reflect his belief in the power of making a positive impact beyond the confines of traditional business, showcasing his commitment to using his resources and influence for the betterment of society.

While Bezos's relentless pursuit of success is undeniable, his perspective on having fun along the way serves as a reminder that true fulfilment arises not only from achieving milestones but also from cherishing the experiences, learnings, and connections forged along the journey. It is this mindset that has allowed Bezos to leave an indelible mark on the world of entrepreneurship, inspiring countless others to embrace the joy of the journey as they strive for their own aspirations. As Bezos once said, "Work hard, have fun, make history."

In Bezos's opinion, festivity and entertainment should be incorporated in our daily life through by any means necessary. Firstly, he encourages individuals and teams to celebrate successes, both big and small. For he believes that by recognizing achievements and milestones, individuals can experience a sense of accomplishment and take pleasure in their progress.

Secondly, Bezos promotes a culture of experimentation and embracing failure as a learning opportunity. He believes that the process of exploration and innovation should be enjoyable and fulfilling in itself, even if the outcome is not always successful. Therefore, by encouraging a mindset of curiosity, risk-taking, and learning, individuals can find joy and satisfaction in the process of discovery.

Bezos also believes in fostering a supportive and inclusive work environment. He encourages teamwork, open communication, and collaboration, where individuals feel valued and respected. By creating a sense of belonging and companionship, organizations can enhance job satisfaction and create an atmosphere where people genuinely enjoy working together.

In addition, Bezos recognizes the importance of maintaining a healthy work-life balance. He believes that individuals should prioritize personal well-being, family, and leisure activities alongside work commitments. Thus, by nurturing personal interests, engaging in hobbies, and spending time with loved ones, individuals can recharge, find inspiration, and bring a sense of joy into their lives.

Ultimately, Bezos encourages individuals to embrace a playful and adventurous mindset. For he believes that by taking on challenges with enthusiasm and a sense of fun can lead to greater creativity and innovation. Thus, by approaching work with a positive and light-hearted attitude, individuals can make their professional journey more enjoyable and fulfilling. So, always remember to enjoy your journey along the way.

Lesson: *Cherish the experiences, learnings, and connections forged along the journey.*

❑

Become Goal Oriented

In the realm of achieving monumental success, the significance of being goal-oriented cannot be overstated. A pivotal figure who embodies this principle in both word and deed is none other than Jeff Bezos, the visionary entrepreneur and mastermind behind the e-commerce behemoth Amazon. Bezos's approach to goal orientation serves as a guiding light for individuals seeking to navigate the intricate path towards their aspirations.

Bezos believes in the power of setting clear goals and working towards them with determination and focus. He understands that having well-defined objectives helps individuals and organizations stay aligned, motivated, and on track to achieve desired outcomes.

In Bezos's view, being goal-oriented involves several key aspects. Firstly, it requires setting ambitious yet achievable goals. Bezos encourages individuals to think big and not be afraid to set bold targets. He often says, "Adapt a 'we are going to conquer the world' mentality." Remember, by aiming high, individuals can push themselves and their teams to reach new levels of achievement.

Secondly, Bezos understands that while setting goals long-term perspective is important. Thus, he encourages individuals to have a clear vision of the future and to set goals that align with that vision. By maintaining a long-term perspective, individuals can prioritize actions and decisions that contribute to sustained success.

Thirdly, Bezos believes in the significance of metrics and measurement to track progress towards goals. He underlines the need for quantifiable metrics that provide clarity and enable individuals to assess their progress objectively. Therefore, by measuring key performance indicators and holding oneself accountable, individuals can ensure they are making meaningful strides towards their goals.

Furthermore, Bezos recognizes the value of prioritization in goal-oriented pursuits. He encourages individuals to identify the most critical goals and allocate time, resources, and attention accordingly. Hence, by focusing on what truly matters and avoiding distractions, individuals can make progress towards their goals more efficiently.

In the end, it is safe to say that by incorporating the essence of Jeff Bezos's philosophy, individuals can infuse their personal goal-setting endeavours with a strategic blend of long-term vision, customer-centricity, adaptability, and single-minded determination.

In short, Bezos's perspective on becoming goal-oriented illuminates the transformative power of setting ambitious objectives and relentlessly pursuing them with unwavering dedication and resilience. Therefore, Jeff Bezos's legacy serves as an inspirational testament to the profound impact that goal orientation can have on shaping a path to unparalleled success. Remember to set high standards for yourself and never settle for mediocrity.

Lesson: *Using metrics is significant to track progress objectively and prioritize critical goals to allocate resources efficiently.*

Be a Team Player

The concept of being a team player lies at the core of any successful organization, resonating with the ethos of collaboration, synergy, and collective achievement. Jeff Bezos symbolizes the essence of effective teamwork and its pivotal role in propelling organizations to unparalleled heights. He believes in the power of collective effort and collaboration. He understands that no individual can accomplish great things alone and that building a strong team is essential for achieving ambitious goals.

According to Bezos, being a team player involves valuing and respecting the contributions of others. He emphasizes the importance of creating a culture that fosters collaboration, open communication, and mutual support. Thus, by embracing diverse perspectives and leveraging the collective intelligence of the team, individuals can drive innovation and make better more informed decisions. One such example of this can be found in the development of the Kindle, where the collaborative efforts of Amazon's teams across various departments led to the creation of a groundbreaking product that revolutionized the e-reading industry.

In addition, on many occasions, Bezos was found appreciating and complimenting his team for their perseverance and contribution to make Amazon a sustained success. Complementing his team, Bezos once said, "Around the world, amazing, inventive, and hard-working Amazonians are putting customers first. I take great pride in being part of this team." He was also found saying that "I get to work with this amazing team of Amazonians all over the world. I am lucky and grateful." Therefore, it essential that you appreciate and support others for their contribution.

One should remember that a team is formed by the integration of individuals with diverse backgrounds, expertise, and skill sets. By harnessing the collective knowledge and perspectives of team members, organizations can benefit from a comprehensive approach to problem-solving and decision-making. This is why, Bezos also encourages individuals to prioritize teamwork over individual ego. Since, he believes in cultivating an environment where everyone feels empowered to share their ideas, take ownership, and contribute to the collective success. Hence, by promoting a culture of collaboration and minimizing internal competition, individuals can work together towards common objectives and accomplish more as a coordinated unit.

Furthermore, Bezos's emphasis on instilling a sense of purpose and shared goals among Amazon's workforce has been instrumental in fostering a cohesive and motivated team. This approach was exemplified during the development and launch of Amazon Web Services (AWS), where cross-functional collaboration and a shared commitment to innovation resulted in the creation of a groundbreaking cloud computing platform that redefined the technological landscape.

Moreover, Bezos recognizes the significance of effective communication within a team. He encourages individuals to actively listen, provide constructive feedback, and encourage open dialogue. So, by fostering an environment where ideas are freely exchanged and feedback is valued, teams can harness the power of diverse perspectives and drive continuous improvement.

Finally, Bezos stresses the importance of accountability and shared responsibility within a team. He believes that each team member should take ownership of their roles and responsibilities while also supporting and helping others. As by holding oneself and others accountable, individuals can foster trust, reliability, and a sense of collective ownership for the team's success.

In short, Jeff Bezos's legacy serves as a timeless testament to the profound influence that effective teamwork can have on shaping the trajectory of organizational success and fostering a culture of perpetual growth and advancement.

Lesson: *Effective teamwork is essential for the success of any organization.*

❑

There Are No Shortcuts

In the fast-paced and competitive world of entrepreneurship and business, the adage that success cannot be achieved through shortcuts holds true. This principle underscores the importance of sustained effort, strategic planning, and a steadfast commitment to long-term goals. In a landscape where innovation and perseverance are paramount, the journey to success demands dedication, resilience, and a steadfast focus on continuous improvement, ultimately culminating in lasting achievements that stand the test of time.

Jeff Bezos believes in the value of putting in the necessary time, effort, and dedication to achieve meaningful results. He notes that there are no quick and easy paths to success. Instead, he encourages individuals to focus on the long-term journey and commit to continuous improvement.

According to Bezos, taking shortcuts often leads to subpar outcomes and missed opportunities for growth. He encourages individuals to embrace the process, embrace challenges, and stay committed to the path of mastery. By investing in learning, skill development, and consistent effort, individuals can build a strong foundation for success.

Bezos also recognizes that setbacks and failures are part of the journey towards success. He advises individuals not to be discouraged by temporary obstacles or setbacks, but rather to view them as opportunities for growth and learning. For instance, Amazon's experience with the Fire Phone, despite its commercial failure, provided crucial insights that later contributed to the success of Amazon's Echo and Alexa devices. Therefore, by persisting through challenges and learning from setbacks, individuals can develop resilience, gain valuable insights, and ultimately move closer to their goals.

Furthermore, Bezos stresses the importance of maintaining a long-term perspective. He recognizes the power of sustained effort and incremental progress over time. Bezos's relentless pursuit of Amazon's long-term vision, despite facing early challenges and setbacks, highlights the life-changing impact of remaining steadfast in the face of adversity and uncertainty. Hence, by focusing on long-term goals and consistently working towards them, individuals can achieve significant results and surpass short-term gains that may come from taking shortcuts.

Moreover, Bezos also encourages individuals to prioritize excellence and customer satisfaction over seeking quick wins. He believes that by delivering exceptional value and continuously improving, individuals can build a strong reputation, gain trust, and establish a foundation for long-term success. So, one should always value excellence over short-term victories.

To summarize, by committing to continuous improvement, embracing challenges, learning from setbacks, and prioritizing excellence, individuals can achieve meaningful and sustained success. Remember as Bezos always says, "You cannot skip or omit steps, you have to put one foot in front of the other, things take time, there are no shortcuts but you want to take those steps with passion and ferocity."

Lesson: *Setbacks and failures are part of the journey towards success, providing opportunities for growth and learning.*

Have Tolerance for Failures

Failures are an integral part of success. It is not wrong to say that every failure is just another stepping stone to eventual success. Therefore, by embracing failure as an integral part of the path to achievement, individuals and organizations can cultivate a mindset that values perseverance, continuous improvement, and the invaluable lessons that arise from navigating challenges and setbacks.

Bezos understands that failure is an inherent part of experimentation and pushing boundaries. He believes that in order to achieve breakthroughs and drive innovation, individuals and organizations must be willing to take risks, which inevitably entails the possibility of failure. This is why, Bezos always says, "As a company grows, everything needs to scale, including the size of your failed experiments. If the size of your failures is not growing, you are not going to be inventing at a size that can actually move the needle."

Also, Bezos once stated that "Failure and invention are inseparable twins. To invent you have to experiment, and if you know in advance that it is going to work, it is not an experiment." So, do not shy away from failures because they are responsible to push you forward towards your ultimate goal.

In Bezos's opinion, having tolerance for failures involves embracing them as learning opportunities rather than viewing them as ultimate setbacks. Thus, he encourages individuals to approach failures with a growth mindset, focusing on the lessons and insights they offer. Hence, by analysing failures, identifying their root causes, and learning from mistakes, individuals can continuously improve and iterate their approaches.

Furthermore, Bezos also recognizes the importance of a long-term perspective when it comes to failure. He believes that setbacks and failures in the short-term should not deter individuals from pursuing their long-term vision. Therefore, by recognizing failures as a stepping stone towards success, individuals can maintain resilience, adapt, and persist in the face of challenges.

Moreover, Bezos promotes a culture that supports risk-taking and learning from failures. He encourages individuals and teams to experiment, take calculated risks, and openly share their learnings. Once Bezos said that "There has to be risk taking. You have to be willing to take risks. You have to be willing to fail." Hence, by fostering an environment that embraces failures as opportunities for growth, organizations can encourage innovation, creativity, and continuous improvement.

Furthermore, Bezos believes in balancing the tolerance for failures with accountability and responsibility. While failures are inevitable, he encourages individuals to take ownership of their actions, learn from their mistakes, and take steps to prevent repeating them in the future. I understand that people sometimes find it hard to take responsibility for their mistakes. But see what Bezos says about mistakes, "I know that we will make mistakes along the way – some will be self-inflicted, some will be served up by smart and diligent competitors. Our passion for pioneering will drive us to explore narrow passages, and, unavoidably, many will turn out to be blind alleys. But with some good fortune there will also be a few that open up into broad avenues." So, by maintaining accountability and a commitment to continuous learning, individuals can grow from failures and drive future success.

In short, by embracing failures as learning opportunities, fostering a culture that supports experimentation and learning, and balancing tolerance with accountability, individuals can navigate failures, drive innovation, and ultimately achieve long-term success. Always remember, failure is just a chance to start anew with greater wisdom and insight.

Lesson: *Failure and invention go hand in hand, and failure should be seen as a learning opportunity rather than a setback.*

❑

Execute Your Ideas

In the dynamic realm of entrepreneurship and innovation, the journey from ideation to execution is paramount. While the birth of groundbreaking ideas lays the foundation, it is the life-changing process of translating these ideas into substantial outcomes that defines the essence of success. The ability to effectively execute ideas into tangible realities reflects the pivotal role of strategic implementation and decisive action in driving substantial impact and fostering sustainable growth within the entrepreneurial landscape.

This is why, Bezos believes that execution is key and that great inspired ideas without proper execution hold little value. He recognizes the need for action and encourages individuals to move forward with determination and a bias for action. Thus, by translating ideas into action, individuals can bring their vision to life and make a tangible impact.

Remember, the execution of the groundbreaking concept of Amazon Prime stands as a testament to Bezos's commitment to transforming innovative ideas into tangible realities. For this reason, in the context of every great idea, Bezos always says, "I knew that if I failed, I would not regret that, but I knew the one thing I might regret is not trying."

According to Bezos, effective execution requires a combination of strategic thinking, planning, and relentless focus on execution. He encourages individuals to break down complex ideas into actionable steps, set clear goals, and develop strong implementation strategies. Hence, by developing a well-defined roadmap and staying disciplined in executing it, individuals can make progress and achieve their desired results.

Also, Bezos recognizes the importance of being adaptable and embracing experimentation during the execution process. He understands that not all ideas will unfold as initially planned, and adjustments may be necessary along the way. Thus, by remaining open to feedback, learning from failures, and iterating on approaches, individuals can refine their execution and increase the chances of success. As Bezos states, "On the details, we at Amazon are always flexible, but on matters of vision we are stubborn and relentless."

Furthermore, Bezos emphasizes the value of taking calculated risks and being comfortable with uncertainties. He recognizes that executing innovative ideas often involves venturing into uncharted territory and facing uncertainty. So, by embracing the unknown, individuals can seize opportunities, learn from challenges, and drive transformative change.

As Edison said, "Ideas without execution are hallucinations." Therefore, without working on your ideas, you cannot achieve success. It is always our actions that set us apart from them crowd. Everyone has unique ideas and thoughts, but only a few work to materialize them. So, execute your ideas because ideas alone will not make you successful and rich.

Lesson: *Execution is key to bringing ideas to life and making a tangible impact.*

❑

Create Great Products

Jeff Bezos has often said, "If you build a great product or service, people will talk about it. But it starts with having something that is worth talking about." This sentiment holds true because creating great products involves more than just offering a solution; it encompasses the art of crafting offerings that seamlessly integrate innovation, user experience, and value, resulting in products that resonate deeply with customers and redefine industry standards.

As a result, Bezos firmly believes that delivering exceptional products is essential for building a successful business. He understands that good products are the foundation of customer satisfaction, loyalty, and ultimately, business growth. Thus, by prioritizing quality, businesses can differentiate themselves, attract customers, and foster long-term success.

In Bezos's view, creating acceptable products starts with a deep understanding of customer needs and preferences. Hence, he emphasizes the significance of being customer-obsessed, which means relentlessly focusing on understanding and exceeding customer expectations. He once said, "We see our customers as invited guests to a party, and we are the hosts. It is our job every day to make every important aspect of the customer experience a bit better." Therefore, gain insight of customer's needs and desires, so businesses can develop products that address their pain points and deliver superior valued products or services.

Bezos also recognizes the importance of continuous improvement and innovation in product development. He encourages businesses to embrace a culture of experimentation and learning. So, by listening to customer feedback, analysing data, and iterating on products, businesses can refine their offerings, enhance features, and stay ahead of evolving customer demands. The launch of the Kindle, Amazon's pioneering e-reader, symbolizes Bezos's commitment to creating innovative products that transform industries and enhance customer experiences. By recognizing the evolving preferences of readers and the need for a portable and user-friendly e-reading device, Bezos and his team successfully developed the Kindle, revolutionizing the way people consume digital content.

Another example of Bezos's relentless pursuit of creating products that redefine convenience and elevate customer satisfaction is the development and evolution of Amazon Prime. By introducing a subscription-based service that offers accelerated shipping, exclusive deals, and access to digital content, Bezos and his team has established a life-changing platform that has not only revolutionized e-commerce but also has redefined the standard of customer-centric offerings within the industry.

Furthermore, Bezos understands that for a business to become successful and have repeating business, it is essential that they build customer trust. Businesses lose potential sales when they fail to establish a meaningingful and deeper connection with prospective buyers. Likewise, when you build trust and loyalty among consumers, it allows you room for more flexibility in decision-making, including the possibility of adjusting prices. Hence, ensuring high-quality products and services is one way to help you get consumers to appreciate and believe in what you have to offer.

As Bezos says, "If you build a great experience, customers tell each other about that. Word-of-mouth is very powerful." According to him, recommendations shared through word-of-mouth can significantly influence the choices consumers make, whether they are buying online or in physical stores. Thus, a company's likelihood of receiving positive reviews, recommendations, and shares among consumers increases as the quality of their product improves.

All in all, building an innovative and unique product or service is pivotal for the success of a business. By infusing product creation with a deep understanding of customer needs, a passion for innovation, and a dedication to delivering exceptional value, individuals or businesses can drive meaningful impact and redefine industries, similarly to Bezos and his team. Remember, exceptional and successful companies are built on the foundation of equally exceptional and innovative products which resonates with their customers need. So, create great and valuable products or services.

Lesson: *Building trust and providing high-quality products and services can lead to positive word-of-mouth recommendation.*

❑

Be a Missionary

Jeff Bezos has always championed the idea of being a missionary, instead of a mercenary. He says that "I strongly believe that missionaries make better products. They care more. For a missionary, it is not just about the business. There has to be a business, and the business has to make sense, but that is not why you do it. You do it because you have something meaningful that motivates you. On the other hand, mercenaries are just trying to make money."

This is why, Bezos has long emphasized the pivotal and seminal role of a missionary mindset in driving the creation of exceptional products. According to him, being a missionary means having a deep sense of purpose and passion for the work one does. It involves being driven by a larger mission or calling beyond just financial gains. Owing to this sentiment, individuals who have a missionary mindset often create products or services that genuinely serve and impact their customers.

In Bezos's opinion, being a missionary entail being customer-obsessed. He understands the importance of prioritizing the needs and desires of customers and striving to exceed their expectations. Thus, by being deeply committed to delivering value and exceptional experiences, individuals can build trust, loyalty, and long-term relationships with customers.

Bezos also encourages individuals to think long-term and make decisions based on the best interests of the mission, even if it means sacrificing short-term gains. He believes that having a missionary mindset involves making choices that contribute to the long-term success and sustainability of the endeavour, rather than solely focusing on immediate profitability.

Furthermore, Bezos recognizes the power of innovation and risk-taking in being a missionary. He encourages individuals to explore new ideas, challenge conventional thinking, and embrace calculated risks in pursuit of the mission. By continuously pushing boundaries, thinking creatively, and adapting to change, individuals can drive innovation and create transformative impact.

Additionally, Bezos acknowledges that the path of a missionary is often marked by challenges, setbacks, and obstacles. Hence, by staying committed to the mission and having the determination to overcome hurdles, individuals can navigate through difficult times and continue making progress.

Therefore, always remember Bezos's word of advice, "Position yourself with something that captures your curiosity, something that you are missionary about." For he believes that missionaries build better products and services. They always win because unlike mercenaries they are not money-motivated. Every mercenary's objective is to make as much money as they can. Yet, paradoxically the missionaries always end up making more than mercenaries. So, work hard and consistently to improve the lives of everyone who comes into your contact. Work for a better and brighter future.

Lesson: *Missionaries build better products and services and ultimately achieve greater success than mercenaries.*

❑

Be Prepared for the Public Attacks

Early in life Jeff Bezos recognized that in the public eye, individuals in positions of influence or leadership are likely to face criticism and attacks. He understands that taking risks, pursuing ambitious goals, and challenging the status quo often invite scrutiny and backlash. Thus, he advises individuals to be prepared for these public attacks and to develop a resilient mindset.

Bezos himself has experienced his fair share of public scrutiny and attacks throughout his career. However, he has repeatedly demonstrated his resilience in dealing with such challenges and finding ways to recover from the effects of criticism on his company. For instance, on Saturday, August 15, 2015, *The New York Times* published an article shedding light on Amazon's business practices. The journalist, Nellie Bowles, portrayed Jeff Bezos, the founder and CEO of Amazon, as a brilliant yet enigmatic and unfeeling corporate titan. It was not the first time when he was called names. In fact, Bezos's public persona was often perceived as mysterious and cold-blooded in his pursuit of success.

In March 2018, another challenge arose for Bezos and Amazon when the US President, Donald Trump, accused the company of various issues, including sales tax avoidance, misuse of postal routes, and anti-competitive practices. This led to negative opinion, causing Amazon's share price to drop by 9 per cent. Consequently, Bezos experienced a significant reduction in his personal wealth, amounting to $10.7 billion.

It is important to note that Bezos and Amazon may not always make decisions that align with public expectations or values. They recognize that even the most accomplished individuals and companies are prone to making mistakes, but when you are successful, your errors may be less easily forgiven or forgotten.

Criticism can be both a blessing and a curse. On one hand, it can serve as a valuable source of feedback, helping entrepreneurs and organizations identify areas for improvement. On the other hand, excessive or unfair criticism can create challenges and even reputational damage. As Bezos says, "If you cannot tolerate critics, do not do anything new or interesting."

Hence, Bezos believes in staying committed to one's goals and not allowing external opinions to derail the pursuit of those objectives. By maintaining a firm belief in the vision and staying focused on the bigger picture, individuals can navigate public attacks with greater resilience.

Bezos also acknowledges the importance of separating personal identity from the attacks themselves. He advises individuals to recognize that criticism is often directed at the role or position they hold, rather than their personal worth. Thus, by developing a mindset that differentiates between attacks on the role and attacks on oneself, individuals can maintain a sense of self-worth and resilience in the face of public scrutiny.

Furthermore, Bezos encourages individuals to learn from criticism and use it as an opportunity for growth. He believes that constructive feedback, even if it comes in the form of public attacks, can provide valuable insights and perspectives. Thus, by being open to feedback and willing to learn from different viewpoints, individuals can adapt, improve, and continue to progress despite public scrutiny.

Additionally, Bezos highlights the importance of building a strong support network. He advises individuals to surround themselves with trusted advisors, mentors, and colleagues who can provide guidance and support during challenging times. Therefore, by leaning on this support system, individuals can find reassurance and encouragement to navigate public attacks.

Basically, to navigate through criticism, successful individuals and businesses must develop the ability to analyze feedback objectively, acknowledging valid concerns and learning from mistakes while also having the courage to defend their actions when appropriate. It is crucial to stay true to one's vision and values, while also being open to constructive feedback that can lead to growth and evolution. As aspiring individuals, learning how to manage criticism with grace and resilience can play a vital and key role in achieving our own success. So, do not let the opinion of others affect you or stop you from making your mark in this world.

Lesson: *Separate personal identity from attacks and learn from criticism for growth.*

❑

Maintain Work-Life Harmony

It seems like everyone is seeking work-life balance these days, and many leaders have even preached about its significance in our everyday life. Jeff Bezos on the other hand does not like the idea of work-life balance. In fact, he completely despises the term "work-life balance" and called the term 'debilitating' in an interview. Instead, he advocates the concept of "work-life harmony". In the interview, he said, "I think work-life harmony is a good framework. I prefer the word 'harmony' to the word 'balance' because balance tends to imply a strict trade-off."

Bezos understands that achieving work-life harmony requires intentional effort and a thoughtful approach. He believes that individuals should strive for a healthy integration of their personal and professional lives rather than viewing them as separate entities in constant conflict. He says that "the reality is, if I am happy at home, I come into the office with tremendous energy and if I am happy at work, I come home with great energy. It actually is a circle. It is not a balance."

Therefore, it is important for all to understand that instead of striving for a strict balance, individuals should aim for a harmonious blend where the energy and enthusiasm from one aspect of life can positively influence the other. Remember, you do not have to make yourself miserable in the pursuit of success.

Consequently, one of the key aspects of Bezos's approach to work-life harmony is to prioritize personal well-being. He stresses on the importance of taking care of oneself physically, mentally, and emotionally. Bezos acknowledges that an individual with a harmonious and gratifying life is better prepared to manage the challenges of work and to make well-informed decisions. Thus, by prioritizing self-care, individuals can bring their best selves to both their personal and professional endeavours.

In Bezos's opinion, it does not matter how much time you spend at home or work. What matters is the energy that you bring to both parts of your life. For instance, if one likes to work long hours and makes them feel energized in return, then by all means they should continue to do so. Likewise, if someone prefer to work flexible hours and spend more time with their loved ones, then so be it. They do not have to feel obliged to work at a 9-5 job if they do not want. At the end of the day, what matters is that you have a fulfilling and purposeful life. Bezos said it right, "You do not have to choose between work and life, you have to strike a harmonious integration."

Additionally, Bezos recognizes the significance of effective time management and prioritization. He advocates for focusing on meaningful tasks that align with long-term goals, while delegating less critical responsibilities. As by doing so, individuals can invest their time and energy in activities that resonate with their purpose and contribute to their overall growth. As he says, "When you talk about decisions and interactions, quality is usually more important than quantity." Hence, it is essential for individuals to schedule their priorities, instead of prioritizing what is on your schedule.

At the end, it is worth noting that achieving work-life harmony is a personal journey, and strategies may vary for different individuals. Though Bezos's insights offer valuable perspectives on the topic, individuals will find it beneficial to explore additional resources and seek personalized advice to develop a work-life harmony strategy that suits their specific circumstances and priorities.

Lesson: *Energy and enthusiasm from one aspect of life can positively influence the other.*

❑

Be Resourceful

Resourcefulness is your ability to find answers to your questions and overcome challenges. It is the one skill that generates all other skills; the talent that ignites all other talents. Developing the skill of resourcefulness is invaluable, whether in personal or professional realms. It not only amplifies productivity but also positions one as an inventive thinker. By fostering resourcefulness, individuals and organizations can enhance their visibility and stay ahead in a competitive landscape, fostering a culture of innovation and adaptability. That is why, Bezos says, "Life is too short to hang out with people who are not resourceful."

According to Bezos, being resourceful is not just about having lots of money or access to abundant resources, but rather making the most of available resources, thinking creatively, and finding unconventional solutions to problems. It involves a mindset of resilience, adaptability, and relentless pursuit of solutions, even when faced with limited resources or constraints.

Bezos encourages individuals to embrace a "do more with less" approach. He believes that constraints can actually foster innovation by forcing individuals to think outside the box and find resourceful solutions. Thus, by leveraging creativity and making efficient use of resources, individuals can achieve remarkable outcomes. Remember, if there is a problem, there is a solution too.

Furthermore, Bezos emphasizes the importance of a customer-centric focus in being resourceful. He believes that truly successful businesses prioritize understanding customer needs and finding efficient ways to meet those needs. Thus, by being resourceful, individuals can identify ways to deliver value to customers in cost-effective and innovative ways.

Bezos also believes that resourcefulness involves taking risks, being willing to try new approaches, and learning from setbacks. By viewing failures as learning opportunities and continuously iterating, individuals can refine their strategies and improve their outcomes.

Moreover, Bezos recognizes that being resourceful involves leveraging the expertise and insights of others. Therefore, by fostering a culture of collaboration, individuals can tap into a broader pool of resources, knowledge, and perspectives, enabling them to achieve more together than they could alone.

In the context of being resourceful, Bezos once observed, "When you are a small company, you have to be resourceful. You have to be more creative. You have to be more innovative." On another occasion he was found saying, "You can achieve anything if you are resourceful." In fact, even Bezos's wife also once said commented that she would rather have a child with nine fingers than one who is not resourceful. Remember, resourceful people are always able to achieve their goals even when faced with challenges or obstacles. After all, it is not about resources but resourcefulness that makes difference in one's life.

Lesson: *Being resourceful is about making the most of available resources, thinking creatively, and finding unconventional solutions.*

❑

Be Curious

From an early age, Jeff Bezos has demonstrated a natural inclination towards curiosity and experimentation. As a young boy, he has eagerly explored the inner workings of objects and transformed his parents' garage into a small experimenting room. This innate curiosity has been manifested in various ways, including his adolescent effort of setting up an electric alarm to protect his personal space from his younger siblings.

Understanding the importance of curiosity, Bezos strongly recommends to cultivate a curious mindset as it is essential for innovation, learning, and staying ahead in this rapidly changing world. Curiosity acts as the lifeblood, fuelling a thirst for knowledge and pushing individuals to push boundaries.

In an interview, Bezos once said, "Position yourself with something that captures your curiosity, something that you are missionary about." He continued, "Keep inventing and do not despair when at first the idea seems crazy. Remember to wander. Let curiosity be your compass."

Bezos firmly believes that curiosity drives exploration and discovery. He encourages individuals to question the status quo, challenge assumptions, and constantly seek new knowledge and insights. Thus, by nurturing a curious mindset, individuals can uncover hidden opportunities, identify emerging trends, and make connections that others may overlook.

Bezos also acknowledges that curiosity fuels creativity and innovation. He emphasizes on the importance of exploring diverse disciplines, industries, and perspectives to stimulate new ideas. By embracing a wide range of interests and continuously learning from various sources, individuals can draw inspiration and develop fresh approaches to problem-solving.

Early in life, Bezos understood that curiosity is closely linked to effective problem-solving. When faced with challenges or obstacles, curious individuals approach them with a sense of inquiry and a willingness to explore multiple perspectives. This open-mindedness and willingness to explore different avenues can lead to more innovative and effective solutions.

In addition, Bezos encourages individuals to have a bias for action when curiosity strikes. He believes that curiosity should be accompanied by a willingness to experiment, take risks, and learn from failures. Therefore, by actively pursuing answers to their questions and putting ideas into action, individuals can gain practical experience, refine their understanding, and foster a culture of innovation.

Another important aspect of curiosity is that in this rapidly changing world, being curious helps individuals to adapt and thrive. Curiosity fosters a mindset of continuous learning and adaptability, allowing individuals to embrace new technologies, trends, and opportunities. It enables them to stay agile and adjust their strategies and approaches to remain relevant and competitive.

In Bezos's opinion, having a builder's mentality is essential for the growth and sustainable success of any business. In one of his annual letters to stakeholders, Bezos has explained the reason behind this belief, "A builder's mentality helps us approach big, hard-to-solve opportunities with a humble conviction that success can come through iteration: invent, launch, reinvent, relaunch, start over, rinse, repeat, again and again. Curious individuals like to invent. Even when they are experts, they are 'fresh' with a beginner's mind. They see the way we do things as just the way we do things now."

In concerns of customer-centricity, Bezos acknowledges that by being genuinely interested in understanding customers' needs, preferences, and pain points, individuals can create better products, services, and experiences. Curiosity about customers' experiences and a commitment to continuously improving those experiences are key drivers of customer satisfaction and business success.

Curiosity also enriches personal development and self-awareness. By exploring different interests and perspectives, individuals gain a deeper understanding of themselves and the world around them. Curiosity encourages self-reflection, introspection, and a continuous quest for personal growth.

Therefore, curiosity is important because it drives learning, fosters innovation, enhances problem-solving skills, promotes adaptability, contributes to personal development, builds relationships, and brings joy and fulfilment. Embracing curiosity empowers individuals to approach life with an open mind, embrace new experiences, and continuously grow and evolve.

Lesson: *Question the status quo, seek new knowledge, and make connections.*

❑

Set Your Priorities

Jeff Bezos, the founder of Amazon, emphasizes the significance of setting priorities for personal and professional success. He believes that setting clear priorities is essential for making effective decisions, managing time efficiently, and achieving meaningful outcomes.

According to Bezos, setting priorities involves determining what truly matters and aligning actions and resources accordingly. It requires identifying the most essential and paramount goals, tasks, or initiatives and focusing on them with intention and discipline.

Bezos advises individuals to be thoughtful and deliberate in setting priorities. He suggests the use of long-term thinking to identify overarching goals and values that guide decision-making. By clarifying priorities, individuals can allocate time, energy, and resources in a way that maximizes productivity and impact.

Furthermore, Bezos encourages individuals to be willing to make trade-offs when setting priorities. Recognizing that time and resources are limited, he suggests identifying and committing to the most critical areas of focus while letting go of less important or distracting endeavours. This deliberate allocation of attention and resources allows individuals to channel their efforts into areas that align with their goals and yield the greatest results.

Bezos also emphasizes the significance of maintaining a customer-centric approach when setting priorities. He believes that prioritizing the needs and preferences of customers is paramount for sustained success. By placing customers at the forefront of decision-making, individuals can ensure that their actions and priorities are aligned with delivering value and exceeding customer expectations.

Additionally, Bezos recognizes the importance of balancing short-term and long-term priorities. While short-term goals may require immediate attention, he advises against neglecting long-term strategic objectives. Therefore, by allocating time and resources to both immediate needs and long-term vision, individuals can foster growth and sustainability.

To conclude, Bezos emphasizes the significance of setting priorities for personal and professional success. By identifying key goals, making trade-offs, and aligning actions with long-term vision and customer needs, individuals can make effective decisions, manage their time efficiently, and achieve meaningful outcomes. Prioritization serves as a guiding principle for focusing efforts, making the most of available resources, and achieving sustainable success in pursuit of personal and organizational goals.

Lesson: *Setting priorities involves identifying what truly matters, aligning actions and resources accordingly, and being deliberate in decision-making.*

❑

Be Stubborn on Your Vision

Jeff Bezos, the visionary founder of Amazon, has often emphasized the importance of being stubborn on your vision. He believes that having a clear and distinctive vision is crucial for achieving long-term success and making a significant impact.

According to Bezos, being stubborn on your vision means maintaining a strong belief in your ideas and staying committed to your long-term goals, even in the face of obstacles, criticism, and setbacks. It involves having the determination and resilience to push forward, despite challenges or naysayers.

One example of Bezos's stubbornness is his decision to invest heavily in Amazon's e-commerce business in the early days, even though it was not yet profitable. Bezos believed that e-commerce was the future of retail, and he was willing to take risks and make sacrifices in order to make it a success. This decision ultimately paid off, as Amazon is now one of the largest and most successful retailers in the world.

Bezos's stubbornness has also been a source of criticism. Some people believe that he is too focused on his own vision and that he is not willing to listen to other people's ideas. However, there is no doubt that Bezos's stubbornness has been a key factor in Amazon's success.

This is why, Bezos encourages individuals to trust their instincts and have the courage to pursue their vision, even when others may doubt or question it. For he believes that truly transformative ideas often face scepticism and resistance in their early stages. By staying true to your vision and persevering through difficult times, you increase the likelihood of realizing your goals and making a meaningful impact.

Additionally, Bezos believes that lasting success often requires taking a patient and persistent approach. Rather than being swayed by short-term fluctuations or external pressures, being stubborn on your vision means remaining focused on the bigger picture and staying committed to the ultimate goal. As Bezos says, "To get something new done, you have to be stubborn, resolute and focused to the point that others might find it unreasonable."

Simultaneously, Bezos also recognizes the need for flexibility and adaptability along the way. While being stubborn about your vision is important, he recognizes that individuals need to be open to feedback, learn from failures, and adjust strategies when necessary. This balance of steadfastness and adaptability allows for continued growth and improvement while staying aligned with the core vision.

Bezos understand that being flexible on details is necessary because as we pursue our vision, along the way we will find that some of our preconceptions were wrong. Thus, we will have to modify our ideas when necessary. It could only be possible when we are flexible on details and are open to make compromises.

Ultimately, it is important that we find harmonious balance of stubbornness and adaptability. After all, Bezos said it right that "If you are not stubborn, you will give up on experiments too soon. And if you are not flexible, you will pound or hit your head against the wall and you will not see a different solution to a problem you are trying to solve." So, be stubborn and uncompromising about your vision, while being flexible on the details.

Lesson: *Acknowledge the need for flexibility and adaptability along the way to achieve success.*

❑

See the Invisible

On August 6, 1991, Sir Tim Berners-Lee accomplished a remarkable feat by publishing the first-ever website on the Internet. At that time, the potential of the World Wide Web was largely unknown, and only a handful of people could envisage the transformative impact it would have on the world.

Merely two years later, in 1993, Jeff Bezos made a bold decision. He resigned from his position as the fourth senior vice president at D. E. Shaw, a prestigious financial firm, to embark on an entrepreneurial journey. Bezos saw the untapped possibilities of the Internet and believed that it could revolutionize how people shop and access information.

With his vision set on creating an online bookstore, Bezos founded Amazon in his garage on July 5, 1994. It was a daring move, especially at a time when the Internet was still in its infancy, and only a fraction of the global population had access to it. Many might have perceived it as an unreasonable endeavour, leaving a stable and promising career to chase after an invisible market.

However, Jeff Bezos's foresight and determination proved to be extraordinary. He understood the power of seeing what others could not yet see. By anticipating the growth and impact of the Internet, he positioned Amazon to become one of the world's largest e-commerce websites.

As a result, Bezos has often spoken about the importance of seeing the invisible as a key mindset for success. He encourages individuals to look beyond what is immediately visible or apparent and to envisage possibilities and opportunities that others may overlook.

Bezos believes that seeing the invisible involves having a strong sense of curiosity, imagination, and a willingness to think differently. It requires the ability to recognize and interpret patterns, trends, and connections that may not be obvious to others. By honing this skill, individuals can uncover hidden potential and uncover new paths to innovation and success.

According to Bezos, seeing the invisible is essential for identifying emerging trends and disruptive opportunities. It involves anticipating future needs and understanding how the world is evolving. Thus, by observing the subtle shifts in customer behaviour, technology advancements, and market dynamics, individuals can position themselves at the forefront of change and make strategic decisions that create a competitive advantage.

To foster the ability to see the invisible, Bezos advises individuals to embrace a growth mindset, stay curious, and surround themselves with diverse perspectives and expertise. He believes that by cultivating an open and flexible mindset, individuals can expand their horizons, challenge their own biases, and unlock new opportunities for personal and professional growth.

Today, Amazon stands as a testament to Bezos's ability to look twenty years into the future and identify opportunities that others overlooked. He went on to become the richest man in the world, amassing tremendous wealth through his innovative approach to business.

Remember, to achieve greatness, we must be willing to challenge conventional thinking, anticipate future trends, and take bold steps towards the seemingly invisible opportunities. The world is constantly evolving, and those who can foresee its trajectory are the ones who will shape it.

As young individuals seeking success, we must ask ourselves, "Where is the world going, and how can I position myself to be at the forefront of that future?" Embracing innovation, harnessing new technologies, and daring to venture into uncharted territories are the keys to unlocking the potential that lies ahead.

Lesson: *To achieve greatness, we must challenge conventional thinking, anticipate trends, and embrace innovation.*

❑

Evolve with Time

To evolve with time means to adapt, grow, and transform in response to changing circumstances, market dynamics, technological advancements, and customer preferences. It involves an ongoing process of innovation, improvement, and adjustment to ensure that a business remains relevant and competitive in a dynamic environment.

Right through his profession, Bezos has demonstrated a keen understanding of the dynamic nature of business and the need for continuous innovation and adaptation. Bezos believes that in today's fast-paced world, it is crucial for individuals and organizations to embrace change rather than resist it. He is aware that market dynamics, consumer preferences, and technology are always changing, and businesses that do not keep up run the risk of becoming irrelevant.

According to Bezos, maintaining a forward-thinking mindset is an essential part of progressing over time. He encourages individuals and organizations to constantly question the status quo, challenge assumptions, and seek out new opportunities rather than resting on previous accomplishments. The ability to spot emerging trends and take advantage of them is made possible by this proactive approach.

In Bezos's view, evolving with time is also essential because customer expectations are constantly evolving. Businesses need to understand their customers' changing needs, preferences, and pain points to deliver value. By evolving with time, businesses can adapt their offerings, customer service processes, and overall strategies to better cater to customer demands. This customer-centric approach helps build customer loyalty, foster positive relationships, and drive customer satisfaction.

Moreover, in a rapidly changing business landscape, agility and adaptability are crucial for survival. Evolving with time allows a business to respond swiftly to market shifts, industry disruptions, and unforeseen challenges. Thus, by staying nimble and responsive, businesses can seize opportunities, navigate obstacles, and remain resilient in the face of adversity.

Ultimately, evolving with time enables a business to achieve sustainable growth. By continuously seeking improvements, exploring new markets, and adapting to change, businesses can expand their customer base, increase market share, and drive long-term success. Evolving with time also positions a business to capitalize on emerging trends and stay ahead of competitors.

As Bezos says, "In business, what is dangerous is not to evolve." Therefore, by staying agile, embracing failure as a learning opportunity, being customer-centric, and taking a long-term perspective, individuals and organizations can navigate the dynamic business landscape and position themselves for continued success in an ever-changing world.

Lesson: *Evolving with time helps businesses understand and cater to evolving customer expectations, build loyalty, and navigate obstacles in a rapidly changing business landscape.*

❑

Fix the Root of the Problem

Fixing the root of a problem means identifying and addressing the underlying causes that give rise to the issue, rather than merely treating its symptoms. It involves delving deep into the core factors that contribute to a problem and implementing solutions that aim to eliminate or mitigate those causes.

Throughout his career, Bezos has shown a relentless focus on identifying and resolving the underlying causes of issues, allowing for more effective and long-lasting solutions. He believes that merely treating the symptoms of a problem can led to temporary fixes that fail to address the core issues. Instead, he encourages individuals and organizations to dig deep and understand the fundamental causes that give rise to the challenges they face. Thus, by tackling these root causes head-on, it becomes possible to implement solutions that bring about true and sustainable change.

According to Bezos, his philosophy of fixing the root of the problem helps in several ways. Firstly, by focusing on the root causes, individuals and organizations can develop solutions that have a lasting impact. Treating symptoms may provide temporary relief, but the problem is likely to recur if the underlying causes remain unaddressed. Fixing the root of the problem ensures that the issue is resolved at its source, leading to more sustainable outcomes.

Secondly, addressing the root causes helps to prevent the problem from recurring in the future. By identifying and eliminating or mitigating the factors that contribute to the issue, individuals and organizations can create a more resilient and stable environment. This proactive approach reduces the likelihood of similar problems arising again.

Furthermore, treating symptoms often involves investing time, effort, and resources repeatedly. On the other hand, fixing the root of the problem may require more upfront investment in terms of analysis, planning, and implementation. However, in the long run, it proves to be more cost-effective and efficient, as it reduces the need for ongoing band-aid solutions and repetitive troubleshooting.

Moreover, Bezos believes that understanding the root causes of a problem provides valuable insights and knowledge that can help make better decisions. It allows individuals and organizations to make informed choices based on a deeper understanding of the issue at hand. By addressing the underlying causes, decision-makers can implement strategies and initiatives that align with the desired outcomes more effectively.

Finally, when the root causes of a problem are identified and addressed, it opens up opportunities for learning and growth. Analysing the underlying factors allows individuals and organizations to gain insights into their processes, systems, and practices. This knowledge can be applied to future endeavours, enabling continuous learning and optimization.

That is why, Bezos urges for fixing the root of a problem rather than treating its symptoms because by focusing on understanding and resolving the underlying causes, individuals and organizations can achieve more effective and lasting solutions.

Lesson: *To be more cost-effective and efficient in the long run. Understand the root cause that provides valuable insights for making informed decisions and opens up opportunities for learning and growth.*

❑

Learn From Your Heroes

Jeff Bezos has consistently emphasized the importance of learning from one's heroes throughout his career. He believes that studying the achievements and approaches of successful individuals can provide invaluable insights and inspiration for personal and professional growth.

Bezos encourages aspiring entrepreneurs and individuals to identify their heroes, whether they are prominent figures or unsung heroes within their fields. These heroes can be individuals who have achieved great success or have made significant contributions in areas of interest. By studying their journeys, analysing their decision-making processes, and understanding the challenges they faced, individuals can extract valuable lessons and apply them to their own lives.

According to Bezos, learning from heroes helps to broaden one's perspective and encourages a long-term mindset. By studying the successes and failures of those who came before, individuals can gain a deeper understanding of the strategies, mindset, and characteristics that contribute to success. This knowledge can serve as a guiding light and help individuals navigate their own paths with greater clarity and purpose.

One of Bezos's key insights is that heroes are not infallible. They too have faced setbacks and made mistakes along the way. By acknowledging their failures and learning from them, individuals can avoid similar pitfalls and make more informed decisions. Bezos himself has often cited figures like Thomas Edison and Walt Disney as sources of inspiration, highlighting their total commitment to innovation and their ability to persevere through challenges.

Learning from heroes also encourages individuals to think big and embrace risk-taking. Bezos believes that studying the achievements of exceptional individuals can push individuals out of their comfort zones and inspire them to dream beyond conventional boundaries. By adopting a growth mindset and embracing calculated risks, individuals can discover new possibilities and push the boundaries of their own potential.

Furthermore, learning from heroes serves as a constant reminder that success is not an overnight phenomenon. Bezos himself has often stressed the necessity of being patient and persistent, emphasizing that meaningful achievements require long-term dedication and resilience. By studying the journeys of heroes, individuals can gain a realistic understanding of the time, effort, and perseverance required to reach their goals.

Therefore, Bezos recommends and underlines the practice of learning from one's heroes as a powerful tool for personal and professional growth. By studying the achievements, strategies, and failures of exceptional individuals, individuals can gain valuable insights, broaden their perspectives, and develop a growth mindset. Learning from our heroes encourages individuals to dream big, embrace risk, and persist in the face of challenges. Ultimately, it is through this process of continuous learning and self-improvement that individuals can increase their chances of achieving greatness in their own endeavours.

Learn: *Learning from heroes pushes individuals to think big, embrace risk-taking, and understand the time and perseverance required for success.*

Do What You Love or Love What You Do

Jeff Bezos, the visionary founder of Amazon, has often shared his perspective on the importance of doing what you love in both personal and professional pursuits. He believes that pursuing one's passion and aligning work with personal interests can lead to greater fulfilment and success.

According to Bezos, when individuals engage in work that they are truly passionate about, they are more likely to invest their time and energy wholeheartedly. This passion fuels motivation, determination, and a strong work ethic, which can contribute to achieving remarkable results.

Bezos encourages individuals to find their true passions and interests, emphasizing that it is worth the effort to discover what truly ignites their enthusiasm. When individuals pursue work that aligns with their passions, it can bring a sense of joy and purpose to their professional lives. This intrinsic motivation can drive individuals to overcome challenges, persist in the face of setbacks, and continuously strive for excellence.

Moreover, Bezos believes that following one's passion fosters innovation and creativity. When individuals are passionate about what they do, they are more likely to think outside the box, challenge the status quo, and explore new possibilities. This mindset of curiosity and exploration can lead to breakthrough ideas and drive entrepreneurial thinking.

However, Bezos also acknowledges that the journey to finding and pursuing one's passion may not always be straightforward. It may require self-reflection, exploration, and a willingness to take risks. He advises individuals to be open to new experiences, to experiment, and to embrace failure as part of the learning process.

Remember that when we do what we love or love what we do than our work becomes more than obligation. Instead, it transforms into a source of joy and fulfilment. This sense of fulfilment not only enhances job satisfaction but also contributes to mental and emotional well-being.

More than this, a genuine passion for one's work often radiates positively in relationships, fostering a positive work environment and stronger connections with colleagues. By doing what we love or loving what we do, individuals can create a high standard and optimistic work culture around them which in turn will keep them inspired along the journey.

In addition, Bezos points out that it is important to note that no matter how passionate we are about our work, there are some aspects of our work that we do not like. For instance, Bezos hates being over scheduled. He insists that he needs some time to think and free himself. For he believes that maintaining a work-life harmony is essential for both professional and personal success. So, do not set yourself for disappointments by demanding life to be perfect always.

Ultimately, be careful when you chose your career because if you do not love what you do or where you are in life than you are likely to feel disconnected, pessimistic, and make more mistakes. So, follow your heart and do what you love. And if it is not possible to do what you love than start appreciating and valuing what you do.

Lesson: *Aligning one's work with their true passions and interests, brings joy and purpose to their professional lives.*

❑

Sleep is Essential

Amazon's and Blue Origin's founder, Jeff Bezos, has always highlighted the importance of personal well-being in the pursuit of success. He has often acknowledged the pivotal role that good quality sleep plays in decision-making, cognitive abilities, and overall health. He believes that getting an adequate amount of sleep is crucial for maintaining mental clarity, creativity, and the ability to handle complex tasks effectively. By prioritizing sleep, individuals can enhance their focus, problem-solving skills, and overall productivity.

Furthermore, Bezos stresses the role of sleep in supporting physical and emotional well-being. He understands that sleep is essential for physical recovery, immune system function, and overall health maintenance. By getting enough restful sleep, individuals can improve their energy levels, mood, and overall quality of life.

In addition, Bezos recognizes that sleep plays a vital role in fostering creativity and innovation. He believes that quality sleep allows the mind to rest, process information, and make connections between ideas. By giving the brain sufficient time to rest and recharge, individuals can experience enhanced creativity and problem-solving abilities.

While the demands of business may tempt individuals to sacrifice sleep in favour of increased work hours, Bezos promotes a harmonious approach. He advocates for setting boundaries, creating a healthy work-life harmony, and ensuring that sleep is prioritized as a non-negotiable aspect of self-care.

It is worth noting that Bezos himself has been known to prioritize a consistent sleep routine. He is often found saying, "I prioritize sleep. I am very focused on it. for me, I need 8 hours of sleep because that is the needed amount for him to feel energized and excited." He continues, "Mostly, as any of us go through our lives, we do not need to maximize the number of decisions we make per day. Making a small number of key decisions well is more important than making many decisions. If you shortchange your sleep, you might get a few extra 'productive' hours, but that productivity might be an illusion. When you talk about decisions and interactions, quality is usually more important than quantity." Thus, by valuing restorative sleep, he demonstrates the recognition that a well-rested mind and body are crucial for sustained success and well-being. It helps prevent individuals to be tired and cantankerous or bad-tempered when making essential decisions and avoid making mistakes. Remember, your work can suffer when you are not well rested.

In fact, even researchers have found a link between adequate sleep and effective leadership. It is said that our performances in daily life are influenced by the quality of our sleep. If we are awake more than 17 to 19 hours than our performance starts to slip the same as someone with a blood alcohol content of 0.05 per cent.

Therefore, it is essential for individuals to establish healthy sleep habits and recognize the value of sleep in achieving sustained success and optimal functioning in both personal and professional endeavours.

Lesson: *Establishing healthy sleep habits is essential for physical recovery.*

❑

Experiment and Then Experiment Again

Jeff Bezos strongly urges the power of experimentation and the continuous pursuit of new ideas. He believes that experimentation is the key to innovation, learning, and long-term success. He says, "To be innovative you must experiment. If you want to have more invention you need to do more experiments per week, per month, per year, per decade. It is that simple. You cannot invent without experimenting."

According to Bezos, the process of experimentation involves taking calculated risks, exploring uncharted territories, and pushing the boundaries of what is known. He says, "One thing about experiments is that many of them fail. After all, if you know it is going to work in advance it is not an experiment."

Bezos firmly believes that failed experiments are a necessary evil that to creating successful invention. Some experiments will succeed, and some may result in failures. However, he affirms that failures and inventions are 'inseparable twins.'

One could not exist without other. This is why, he encourages individuals and organizations to embrace failure as a natural part of the experimentation process, recognizing that it often leads to valuable lessons and insights.

Unfortunately, most often if not always businesses and individuals do not embrace failures and consider them as setbacks. In an interview, Bezos once commented on this very nature of businesses that "most large organizations embrace the idea of invention, but they are not willing to suffer the string of failed experiments necessary to get there." Remember as any organization grows, the size and amount of the mistakes must grow as well. Because if it does not, then they are not going to be inventing at scale that can move the needle.

Moreover, Bezos believes that through experimentation, individuals can uncover new opportunities, challenge assumptions, and discover groundbreaking solutions. He emphasizes the importance of maintaining a culture that encourages and rewards innovation, curiosity, and a willingness to try new approaches.

Furthermore, Bezos encourages a cycle of continuous experimentation. For he believes that successful organizations should not rest on past achievements but should constantly strive to improve and innovate. This involves continually testing hypotheses, gathering data, and iterating based on feedback. Thus, by embracing this iterative process, individuals and organizations can make incremental improvements, adapt to changing circumstances, and stay or remain ahead of the competition.

Additionally, Bezos also encourages individuals to have a long-term perspective when it comes to experimentation. He believes that the benefits of successful experiments may not always be immediate, and patience is often required. Thus, by focusing on long-term goals and being willing to invest time and resources into experimentation, individuals can lay the foundation for transformative breakthroughs and sustainable growth.

Lastly, Bezos encourages individuals and businesses to grow a thick skin and be willing to be misunderstood for a long time. For he says, "Invention requires a long-term willingness to be misunderstood. If you really have conviction that others are not right then you need to have that long-term willingness to be misunderstood."

However, one should also know when to stop experimenting, especially when they are not assisting you to invent new opportunities. At times like this, it is not wrong or bad to put a stop on such experiments. Remember as Bezos says, "On the day you decide to give up on them, what happens? Your operating margins rise or go up because you stopped investing in something that was not working. Is that really such a bad day?" So, experiment and then experiment again till they help you make invention.

Lesson: *Experimentation involves taking calculated risks and exploring uncharted territories.*

❑

Have a Long-term Perspective

Jeff Bezos was often found saying, "If we think long-term, we can accomplish things that we could not otherwise." For he believes that having a long-term perspective is crucial for driving sustainable growth and making a meaningful impact. He understands that short-term gains should not compromise long-term value creation and customer satisfaction.

Bezos has always urged that one of the core principles for Amazon's and his success is their loner-term thinking than most companies. According to Bezos, many companies often give up on an idea if it does not produce returns in quarter or year. Yet, in Amazon Bezos and his team sticks with an idea or initiative for five, six, seven years—all the while keeping the investment manageable, constantly learning, and improving—till it gains momentum and acceptance.

The prime example of Bezos's and Amazon's long-term perspective is Amazon Prime Video, which has more than 100 million viewers. It is the result of decades of research, development, and content acquisition. Imagine, if Bezos and his team at some point has given up on this idea, then may be today we might not be enjoying its services. That is why, it is essential to have a long-term perspective if you want to create something big and enduring.

In 2017, during the Internet Association's annual gala, Bezos said, "When you run a corporation with a market cap over a trillion dollar like Amazon, having a long-term thinking approach helps businesses focus on planning and where they should invest their energy."

Now, it is crucial to understand that a long-term perspective requires resisting the temptation of quick wins or immediate gratification. Therefore, Bezos encourages individuals and organizations to focus on long-term goals and investments that may take time to materialize. Because by avoiding short-term thinking, individuals can make decisions that prioritize long-term value over short-term gains. Bezos understands that short-term gains are not sustainable and thus he aims to create a business model that can withstand the test of time.

Moreover, Bezos has proved that by implementing a long-term approach, individuals and businesses can maintain a competitive edge and drive sustained growth in the market. Thus, by adopting the long-term approach, only then will you disrupt your competitors but also influence the market landscape by setting new standards for competition.

Also, Bezos encourages individuals to think in terms of decades, not just years or quarters. He believes that truly transformative and impactful endeavours require sustained effort and commitment. By embracing a long-term mindset, individuals can set audacious goals, invest in innovation, and persevere through challenges with the understanding that lasting and enduring success often takes time to achieve.

Additionally, Bezos firmly believes that a long-term perspective is essential for fostering a culture of innovation. He encourages employees to think big and take risks, even if it means failing in the short-term. This culture of innovation has been a key driver of Amazon's success, leading to the development of groundbreaking products and services such as Amazon Prime, Amazon Web Services, and the Kindle.

Therefore, by adopting long-term perspective, individuals and businesses can make bold decisions, invest in research and development, and create innovative products and services that meet the needs of customers.

Lesson: *Constantly learn and improve until it gains momentum and acceptance.*

❑

Be a Good Storyteller

In today's golden age of internet, Bezos believes that storytelling is an essential skill for entrepreneurs and leaders. He understands that the power of storytelling can be used in conveying ideas, connecting with others, and inspiring action. He recognizes that compelling narratives can engage people emotionally and intellectually, making information more memorable and impactful.

In Bezos's view, storytelling allows entrepreneurs to effectively convey their ideas and passion to others, making it easier to attract investors, build a strong team, and create a successful business. He believes that a well-crafted story can capture the essence of a company's mission and values, making it more relatable and memorable to both employees and customers.

Bezos observes how in Amazon instead of relaying on PowerPoints or Slide presentations, they write narratively structured six-page memos and silently read one at the beginning of each meeting in a study hall. He says, "These memos generally range from one to six pages and articulate the project goal(s), approach to addressing it, outcome, and next steps. Given this unique aspect of our culture, and the impact these papers have on what decisions we make as a company, being able to articulate your thoughts in written format is a necessary skill."

Remember that storytelling is a skill that humans has been using from thousands and thousands of years. It is through storytelling that we exchange and deliver knowledge from one person to millions. One of the prime examples of Bezos's storytelling philosophy are the annual letters that he has been writing to the stakeholders of Amazon since 1997. In his letters, he often narrates his vision for what Amazon will going to become.

According to Bezos, to become a competent storyteller involves several key aspects. Firstly, it requires the ability to craft a clear and compelling narrative. He believes that by framing ideas within a well-developed story, individuals can capture attention and communicate their vision effectively.

Secondly, Bezos recognizes the value of authenticity in storytelling. He believes that sharing personal experiences, insights, and lessons learned can make stories more relatable and engaging. Thus, by connecting on a human level and revealing the motivations behind their ideas, individuals can establish trust and build a connection with their audience.

Furthermore, Bezos encourages individuals to leverage visuals, data, and anecdotes to enhance their storytelling. He understands that incorporating visual elements and compelling examples can make stories more vivid and memorable. Therefore, by appealing to both the logical and emotional aspects of the audience's mind, individuals can leave a lasting impression and effectively convey their messages.

Moreover, Bezos highlights the importance of simplicity and clarity in storytelling. He believes that complex ideas can be distilled into simple and compelling narratives that resonate with a wide range of audience. Hence, by avoiding technical terminology, using relatable language, and focusing on key messages, individuals can make their stories more accessible and impactful.

Additionally, Bezos recognizes the value of practising and refining storytelling skills. He understands that effective storytelling is a craft that can be honed over time. Thus, by seeking feedback, observing other skilled storytellers, and continuously practising the art of communication, individuals can enhance their storytelling abilities and engage audiences more effectively.

Remember, storytelling is important for several reasons. For instance, it helps to create a shared vision among team members. When people understand the 'why' behind a project, they are more likely to be motivated and engaged. Storytelling can also help to build trust and credibility with customers and stakeholders. When people feel that they understand the company's story, they are more likely to trust it and do business with it. Likewise, storytelling can help to differentiate a company from its competitors. Therefore, by creating a unique and compelling story, a company can stand out from the crowd and attract more customers. So, practice and hone your storytelling skills if you wish to become successful in both personal and professional life.

Lesson: *Storytelling creates a shared vision, builds trust, credibility, and differentiates companies from competitors.*

❑

Protect Our Planet

The natural world is an incredible wonder of this universe. It forms the very foundation of our economy, society, and even our fundamental existence. We get our food, our air, and the water we use to irrigate our crops from our forests, rivers, oceans, and soils. We also depend on them to provide us several other resources and services. Thus, nature is an indispensable part of our existence. Without it, we cannot survive in this universe.

Due to our past careless actions, today the world is suffering from various changes that are causing risk to its very existence. Many species and resources are becoming extinct and climate is changing its course rapidly. In many parts of the world, the nature is already suffering from carbon sink to a carbon source. Thus, understanding nature's significance, Bezos has committed to protect our planet and help it restore its previous healthy state or at least prevent it from further degradation.

On November 2, 2021, at the COP26 climate summit, Bezos has pledged $3 billion in funding to help restore nature and transform food system. Addressing the audience, he said, "In this decisive decade, we must all stand together to protect our world." He further continued, "We must conserve what we still have. We must restore what we have lost. And we must grow what we need to live without degrading the planet for future generations to come."

According to Bezos, nature is beautiful but it is also fragile. Knowing this, we all must ask ourselves that do we want to preserve the very essence of the nature and let our future generation have the chance to experience an improving natural world. Naturally, the answer would be yes. Therefore, we must all do our best to protect the mother nature. Remember, even the smallest acts to conserve nature can improve the world better.

Bezos believes that investing in nature through both traditional and innovative approaches is essential to combat climate change, enhance biodiversity, protect the beauty of the natural world, and create a prosperous future. He understands that with several resources in hand, the entrepreneurs have the power and opportunity to contribute a significant amount of assistance in protecting our planet.

For instance, the entrepreneurs could help by reducing industrial waste, using eco-friendly materials, and minimizing the carbon footprint of operations. Also, they could develop and promote products and services that are environmentally-friendly. Another way with which entrepreneurs could help the natural world is by collaborating with environmental organizations and participating in conservation initiatives.

One of the most notable initiatives of Jeff Bezos to protect our planet is "The Bezos Earth Fund." This fund was created by Bezos with the commitment of $10 billion from Bezos in 2020 to be disbursed as grants to address climate and nature within the current decade. Another illustration of Bezos's commitment to preservation of Earth is Blue Origin, which was founded by

Bezos with the vision of millions of people living and working in space for the benefit of the earth.

Remember, it is essential that we all must work collaboratively to lessen or reduce the causes of climate change, adapt to its impact, and build a more sustainable and resilient for the planet.

Lesson: *The natural world is vital for our economy, society, and existence.*

❑

Disagree and Commit

According to Bezos, when an individual comes up with an idea that he/ she are in love with and want to see it pursued, then the first thing they must do is to build a support system for it. For this they will need a team of smart, pragmatic and wise individuals to accept the idea and move it forward.

In Amazon, Bezos and his team use a unique framework called "Disagree and Commit." This framework encourages individuals to openly discuss the idea within a team or organization to decide if they should pursue a particular idea or not. This approach allows the individuals to disagree while making the decision, but once the decision is made then everybody in the team must commit to implement the decision.

This is why, in Amazon, Bezos's team does not have fully convince on a particular project or idea. Rather, all they must do is convince him enough to be willing to let them move forward with the said project or idea. Once he agrees to move forward with an idea, Bezos is always willing to fully commit to the vision of his team, even if he does not support their vision. Similarly, if anyone within the team disagree with a particular project or idea, they must still commit to that project or idea and work with the team to let it come to fruition.

Bezos points out that not being willing to fully commit to a particular project or idea means sabotaging the team and wastage of time and money. Therefore, for the success of a project or idea, it is crucial that individuals commit completely to the team's vision, even when they do not agree with the vision.

Often when Bezos is keen on an idea but his team does not share his vision, he would say to them, "I want you to gamble with me on this." He would use this phrase at times when he himself is not sure of what the right answer is but still feels strongly about that idea.

Bezos urges that the "Disagree and Commit" framework has several advantages. For instance, it helps create an environment where different perspectives are considered and valued. Also, it acknowledges that not everyone will always agree on every decision. In addition, it helps discourage prolonged debates and indecisiveness. Lastly, regardless of initial disagreements, team members are united in supporting and working towards the success of the chosen vision.

Therefore, the "Disagree and Commit" framework is a useful framework that ensures 100 per cent commitment of all team members to a particular project or idea.

Lesson: *Promote diverse perspectives and discourage prolonged debates.*

❑

Manage Your Time Better

With a limited amount of time in our possession, it is crucial that we make use of this finite resource effectively without wasting it in meaningless endeavours. Understanding its value Bezos emphasizes on using it wisely to achieve personal and professional success in one's life. This is why, Bezos recognize the need to prioritize tasks and allocate time wisely to maximize productivity and achieve desired outcomes.

One of the richest men of the world, Jeff Bezos does not waste his valuable time in unnecessary and big meetings. He has his own philosophy to micromanage his effectively and efficiently. He calls it "two pizza rule." In Bezos's opinion, no meeting should be too big. In fact, he refuses to attend any meeting that consists of too many people. Now, question is how he determines how much is too many? The answer is simple. If two pizzas cannot feed the amount of people that are suppose to go to a meeting, then it is too big. Like Bezos, many of the successful entrepreneurs have their own strategies and time management system to effectively use their time. Such as "Time

Blocking" method of Elon Musk, "The Two Minute" rule of David Allen, and so on.

According to Bezos, there are several aspects that are crucial in effective time management. Firstly, individuals are required to set clear goals and define priorities. Thus, Bezos encourages individuals to identify the most important tasks or objectives and focus on those that align with their long-term vision. This will help individuals to allocate their time and energy accordingly.

Secondly, Bezos asks individuals to effectively plan and organize their daily schedule. He recognizes the power of proactive scheduling and structuring one's day to optimize productivity. Therefore, by planning ahead, breaking down tasks into manageable chunks, and creating a structured framework, individuals can make the most of their time and minimize inefficiencies.

Thirdly, Bezos emphasizes the significance of minimizing distractions and staying focused. He encourages individuals to eliminate or reduce interruptions that can derail their productivity. This may involve setting boundaries, managing digital distractions, and creating an environment conducive to concentration. Thus, by maintaining focus on the task at hand, individuals can accomplish more in less time.

Furthermore, Bezos promotes the delegation of tasks to trusted team members. He believes in leveraging the strengths and expertise of others to free time for higher-value activities. Delegating tasks that others can handle effectively allows individuals to focus on strategic decision-making and activities that align with their core responsibilities.

Additionally, Bezos encourages individuals to adopt a disciplined approach to time management. He understands the importance of maintaining a routine, establishing productive habits, and avoiding procrastination. Hence, by practising discipline and consistently adhering to planned schedules and routines, individuals can increase productivity and make the most of their time.

Remember to manage your time appropriately because once gone it will be forever lost to you.

Lesson: *Use time wisely, as once it is gone, it cannot be regained.*

❑

Be Willing to Take Risks

In today's fast paced and competitive world, being willing to take risks is a necessity and not an option. If individuals and businesses are not willing to take risks in life and business then they are already done for because without risk it is not possible for anyone to achieve greatness and success. Without risk or making bold decisions, you will end up living a mediocre life and become stagnant.

This is why, Bezos always encourages individuals and businesses to take risks and make bold decision. For he understands that innovation inherently involves uncertainty and often we will fail in our endeavours. But without getting out of our 'safe' or 'comfort' zone we will not be able to explore the uncharted territories and discover the unknown. Therefore, it is crucial for us to courageously step out of comfort zones so that we could make great discoveries.

Remember, if the Wright brothers or Thomas Edison had not taken bold decisions and went against what others said, then today we might not be experiencing the wonders of aeroplanes and electricity respectively. It is understandable that you will face opposition and ridicule from others when you will propose ideas beyond their understanding. It is also inevitable to avoid failures on the path of success.

The reason behind Bezos's and Amazon's success is his willingness to take calculated risks in both business and life. After all, years ago if he had not made the bold decision of quitting his well-earning job to sell books online then we would be deprived of Amazon today. Another notable example of Bezos's risk-taking is Amazon's early investment in cloud computing. In 2006, Amazon launched Amazon Web Services (AWS), which provides cloud computing services to businesses and individuals. At the time, cloud computing was a relatively new concept, and many were sceptical about its potential. However, Bezos believed that cloud computing would revolutionize the way businesses operate, and he was willing to invest heavily in its development. Today, AWS is one of the most successful cloud computing platforms in the world, and it has been a major driver of Amazon's growth.

Similarly, Bezos has taken the risk to invest in space exploration through his company, Blue Origin. Blue Origin develops reusable rockets and other technologies that could make space travel more affordable and accessible. Though it is a highly ambitious and risky endeavour, Bezos believes that it is important to invest in the future of space exploration.

In the rapidly involving world, not taking any risk is the biggest risk in life. Remember, risk-taking is fundamental to innovation. Bezos sees risk-taking as a source of competitive advantage, allowing individuals and businesses to explore new markets and disrupt traditional industries. As Bezos says, "If you are not taking risks, then you are not moving forward." Thus, to grow and achieve sustained success, it is essential for us to take risks and make some bold decisions in life and business.

However, Bezos stresses on taking calculated risks rather than just making stupid and irreversible decisions. It is crucial to understand that when we talk about taking risks and making bold decisions then we are talking making decisions after much deliberation and carefully analysing the relevant information, data, and consequences. After all, we want you to be courageous not reckless. So, take calculated risks that aligns with your strategic vision and objectives.

Lesson: *Understand the importance of taking calculated risks rather than reckless ones.*

❑

Understand Your Business

Jeff Bezos emphasizes the value of diving deep into understanding your business or work because he believes that understanding your business goes beyond surface-level knowledge and it involves having a deep comprehension of the various components that drive your organization. It encompasses understanding your business model, target market, competitive landscape, internal operations, financials, and overall strategic direction. This level of understanding of your business or work is crucial because it provides a foundation for informed decision-making and successful business management.

Bezos advocates to gain a comprehensive understanding of one's business and he encourages individuals to dig deeper, ask critical questions, and seek a deeper level of insight. By diving deep, individuals can uncover hidden opportunities, identify potential challenges, and make more informed judgments. He says, "If you do not understand the details of your business, you are going to fail."

According to Bezos, understanding your business or work deeply have several benefits. Firstly, understanding your business allows you to make informed decisions. By having a clear understanding of your organization's goals, values, and unique selling propositions, you can make strategic choices that align with your vision and objectives. This understanding helps you identify the right opportunities to pursue, evaluate risks, and allocate resources effectively. Without a comprehensive understanding of your business, decision-making becomes disorganized and lacks strategic direction.

Secondly, understanding your business helps you identify opportunities for growth. By analysing your target market, customer needs, and emerging trends, you can identify gaps in the market that your business can capitalize on. Understanding your competitive landscape enables you to differentiate your offerings and develop competitive advantages. It also helps you identify potential partnerships, collaborations, or acquisitions that can propel your business forward. Without a solid understanding of your business and the market, you may miss out on growth opportunities or fail to adapt to changing market dynamics.

Thirdly, understanding your business is vital to alleviate risks. By thoroughly understanding your financials, operational processes, and potential vulnerabilities, you can identify and address areas of risk. This allows you to implement risk management strategies, develop contingency plans, and ensure business continuity. Without a deep understanding of your business, you may overlook critical risks, leading to financial losses, reputational damage, or operational disruptions.

Furthermore, understanding your business fosters effective resource allocation. By having a clear understanding of your organization's capabilities, strengths, and weaknesses, you can allocate resources, including finances, talent, and technology, in a manner that optimizes their impact. This helps avoid wasting resources on ventures that do not align with your business objectives or do not leverage your core competencies.

Finally, understanding your business enhances communication and alignment within your organization. When all stakeholders, including employees, partners, investors, and customers, have a shared understanding of your business, it facilitates effective collaboration, teamwork, and customer engagement. It helps create a common language and vision, ensuring that everyone is working towards the same goals.

Therefore, if you are not well-versed of informed about your business or job then the probability of your failure is high. So, before starting a new venture, commit yourself to learn and understand the minute details of your business.

Lesson: *Without a comprehensive understanding of your business, decision-making becomes disorganized and lacks strategic direction, and you may miss out on growth opportunities or fail to mitigate risks effectively.*

❑

Have a High Standard Culture

Jeff Bezos has long been an advocate of fostering a high and elevated standard culture within Amazon, stressing the importance of maintaining excellence and embracing a relentless pursuit of customer satisfaction and operational efficiency. He has often highlighted the significance of setting ambitious goals and holding oneself to exceptionally high standards, both in terms of products and customer service.

Bezos firmly believes that a high standard culture is not just about meeting customer expectations but about continually surpassing them and exceeding what is thought possible. This sentiment is reflected in his well-known quote, "We see our customers as invited guests to a party, and we are the hosts. It is our job every day to make every important aspect of the customer experience slightly better."

In 2017, in his annual letter to stakeholders, Bezos wrote, "Building a culture of high standards is well worth the effort, and there are many benefits. Naturally and most obviously, you are going to build better products and services for customers—this should be reason enough. Perhaps a little less obvious: people are drawn to high standards—they help with recruiting and retention. More subtle: a culture of high standards is protective of all the 'invisible' but crucial work that goes on in every company. I am talking about the work that no one sees. The work that gets done when no one is watching. In a high standards culture, doing that work well is its own reward – it is part of what it means to be a professional. Finally, high-standards are fun! Once you have tasted high standards, there is no going back."

Furthermore, Bezos's commitment to high standards is reflected in his insistence on prioritizing long-term customer satisfaction over short-term gains. Despite the intense pressure from investors for short-term profits, Bezos has consistently reinvested a considerable or appreciable portion of Amazon's revenue back into the company, focusing on expanding its product offerings, improving customer experiences, and implementing cutting-edge technology to enhance operational efficiency.

Now the question arise that what do you need to achieve high standards in a particular domain area? Bezos has an answer for this too. According to him, first, you have to be able to recognize what looks good in that particular domain. Second, you must have realistic expectations for how much work it will take to achieve that result—the scope.

Bezos has explained the importance of realistic expectations when it comes to achieving high standards by using the example of handstand. He says, "Most people think that if they work hard, they should be able to master a handstand in about two weeks. The reality is that it takes about six months of daily practice. If you think you should be able to do it in two weeks, you are just going to end up quitting. Unrealistic beliefs on scope – often hidden and undiscussed – kill high standards. To achieve high standards yourself or as part of a team, you need to form and proactively communicate realistic beliefs about how tough or difficult something is going to be."

Moreover, Bezos emphasizes that high standards are teachable. When you are around people who have high standards, you tend to pick up those standards too. It is like catching a good habit from someone. If you join a team that aims for excellence, you will naturally start aiming for the same. On the other hand, if a team has low standards, that attitude can spread too.

Therefore, by setting and maintaining high standards, organizations can create a culture of excellence that drives exceptional performance and continuous growth. Bezos's perspective highlights the significance of fostering a culture that embraces high standards as a foundation for success.

Lesson: *Building a culture of high standards has numerous benefits, including better products & services, retaining talented individuals, and valuing the invisible work done behind the scenes.*

❑

Don’t Wish for a Fair Fight

Jeff Bezos, the founder of Amazon, recognizes that wishing for a fair fight is not always the most effective approach. More often in life, if not always, you will find yourself at a disadvantage. After all, life is not fair to everyone. So, when you find yourself at a disadvantage or when things are not equal, it is fine or acceptable to use your own special skills or advantages to make things fairer for you.

This is why, Bezos believes in seeking and leveraging asymmetrical advantages in business. He understands that in a competitive landscape, aiming for a fair fight can limit potential success. Instead, he encourages individuals and organizations to identify their unique strengths, exploit market opportunities, and create their own advantages.

Jeff Bezos, the founder of Amazon, did not simply enter the market and compete directly with established brick-and-mortar retailers on their terms. Instead, he leveraged technology and innovation to create a definite advantage for Amazon. He is a perfect example of how to leverage asymmetrical advantages in business.

For instance, when Amazon started, traditional bookstores were already established and seemingly dominating the market. Rather than trying to compete with them head-on, Bezos took a different approach. He recognized the potential of the internet early on and saw an opportunity to create an online platform that would revolutionize the way people buy books and later all kinds of products. He used the internet's vast reach and efficiency to offer an extensive selection of books at competitive prices, providing customers with a convenient and hassle-free shopping experience.

Furthermore, as Amazon expanded, Bezos did not confine the company to just being an online bookstore. He strategically diversified its offerings, incorporating various products and services, including e-readers, cloud computing, and streaming services. This diverse approach allowed Amazon to become a dominant force in the e-commerce industry, and subsequently in multiple other sectors.

Additionally, Bezos underlined the importance of embracing disruptive technologies rather than fearing them. He supported the introduction of the Kindle e-reader, which helped revolutionized the publishing industry, challenging traditional book publishing models and establishing Amazon as a prime player in the e-book market.

Another example of seeking and leveraging asymmetrical advantage in Bezos's life is cloud computing. Amazon Web Services (AWS), Amazon's cloud computing division, was not a direct area of expertise for the company initially. However, Bezos recognized the potential of cloud computing early on and invested heavily in developing AWS. This move not only helped Amazon in diversifying its business portfolio but also allowed the company to gain a significant advantage over its competitors in the cloud services market.

Thus, the quote "don't wish for a fair fight" embodies Bezos's strategy of not merely trying to compete on an even playing field, but rather creating a new battlefield, leveraging technology, innovation, and diversification to gain a significant advantage. Bezos focused on transforming the rules of the game, ultimately redefining the retail landscape and setting Amazon on the path to becoming one of the most valuable companies in the world.

Therefore, always remember that by seeking unique strengths, challenging the status quo, and creating their own advantages, individuals can position themselves for success and outperform competitors.

Lesson: *Create new battlefields and transform the rules of the game!*

❑

Dominate the World

Amazon's success has been transformative in the e-commerce space. They have revolutionized online shopping, making it more convenient and accessible for billions of people worldwide. Under Bezos guidance, Amazon grew from an online bookstore into the world's largest e-commerce platform, offering a vast array of products and services. Amazon's vast product selection, competitive pricing, and efficient delivery have set new industry standards.

However, Jeff Bezos is not only associated with the success of Amazon but has also been a strategic investor in several other companies. One notable example is his early investment in Google. In 1998, Bezos invested $250,000 in Google, becoming one of its first shareholders. This initial investment resulted in him acquiring 3.3 million shares of Google stock, which was valued at about $3.1 billion in 2017.

Apart from Google, Bezos has been involved in other ventures as well. He was one of the investors in Segway, a company launched in 1999 that aimed to revolutionize personal transportation. Additionally, in September 2000, Bezos founded Blue Origin, a human spaceflight startup company. Blue Origin's mission revolves around advancing space exploration and the potential for human life in the solar system.

Furthermore, in 2006, Amazon's innovations in cloud computing through Amazon Web Services (AWS) have had a profound impact on the tech industry, providing essential infrastructure for businesses, startups, and developers around the globe. Their efficient supply chain and use of data-driven insights have been a game-changer in the industry.

Moreover, as Amazon expanded, it created several job opportunities for millions of people, both directly and indirectly through its third-party seller network. It has had a tremendous economic impact on communities and regions where it operates.

According to Bezos, world domination is paramount in business for several reasons. Firstly, businesses that dominate the world enjoy a leading competitive advantage over their rivals. This leadership position allows them to shape market trends, set prices, and dictate the direction of the industry. They become the go-to choice for consumers and businesses alike, cementing their place as the preferred option in the marketplace.

Secondly, dominant businesses often contribute significantly to economic growth and job creation. They have the resources to invest in research and development, infrastructure, and human capital, driving innovation and productivity gains. As they expand, they generate employment opportunities and stimulate economic activity in their home countries and beyond.

In addition, Bezos recognize that world-dominating businesses are often at the forefront of innovation. They invest heavily in research and development, pushing the boundaries of technology and disrupting traditional industries. Their innovations have far-reaching impacts, from transforming daily life to addressing global challenges.

Lastly, Bezos acknowledges that dominant businesses have the capacity to make a positive impact on society and the environment. They can lead by example in sustainable practices, philanthropy, and social initiatives, setting the standard for corporate responsibility. This is the reason why, Bezos founded Blue Origin.

Ultimately, dominating the world in business means achieving an unparalleled level of success, influence, and impact. Such dominance is essential for market leadership, economic growth, innovation, and global reach. As world-dominating businesses shape industries and economies, they carry a responsibility to act ethically, drive positive change, and inspire future generations of entrepreneurs. Therefore, the pursuit of dominance should always align with a commitment to sustainability, responsibility, and making a meaningful contribution to the world.

Lesson: *Dominating the world in business brings competitive advantage, economic growth, innovation, and the opportunity to make a positive impact on society and the environment.*

❑

Working Backwards Method

We are all aware that Jeff Bezos has always been known for his innovative thinking and strategic approach to business. One of the key methodologies he believes that is responsible for his success is the "Working Backwards" method. This approach involves starting with the customer and their needs, and then working backwards to develop products and services that fulfill those needs. According to Bezos, this method is essential for driving innovation and ensuring customer satisfaction.

The Working Backwards approach is based on the idea that understanding the customer's requirements and expectations is crucial to building successful products and services. Bezos believes that companies should prioritize customer needs over internal processes or existing structures. By starting with the customer, businesses can align their efforts and resources to deliver the best possible solutions. The "Working Backwards" conveys the company's exhausting focus first and foremost on customer satisfaction.

Amazon's Working Backwards method is also known as PR/FAQ method. Here, PR means Press Release and FAQ means Frequently Asked Questions. In this method, there are two essential steps. The first step is to create a hypothetical press release or product description that outlines the customer experience. This document serves as a clear and concise vision of what the final product will look like and how it will benefit customers. By creating this narrative upfront, the team gains a shared understanding of the goals and outcomes they want to achieve.

Once the press release is established, the next step is to write a Frequently Asked Questions (FAQ) document. This document helps the company to anticipate and address potential questions or concerns that customers may have about the product. It also assists in clarifying the features, functionality, and value proposition of the offering. Writing the FAQ document requires deep thinking and a comprehensive understanding of the customer's perspective.

The Working Backwards method encourages teams to think in a customer-centric manner throughout the product development process. It helps to avoid the common pitfall of focusing solely on the internal aspects of the business or getting carried away with technical details. By continuously referring back to the Press Release and FAQ document, teams can ensure that their decisions align with the desired customer experience.

As Bezos says, "The Working Backwards Process is not designed to be easy; it is designed to save a vast amount of work on the backend and to ensure we are building the right thing." According to him, "Working backwards from customer needs often demands that we acquire new competencies and exercise new muscles, never minding how uncomfortable and awkward-feeling those first steps might bring."

Bezos believes that the Working Backwards approach helps avoid "one-way doors" or irreversible decisions that can have significant consequences on one's business. By investing time and effort upfront to clearly define the customer's needs and the desired outcome, companies can avoid costly mistakes and course corrections later in the development process.

Furthermore, the Working Backwards method promotes a culture of innovation and experimentation within organizations. It encourages teams to think creatively and challenge conventional wisdom. By focusing on the customer and their needs, companies can uncover new opportunities and develop groundbreaking solutions that disrupt existing markets.

In an interview, Bezos attributed much of Amazon's success to the Working Backwards method. He said, "There are two ways to extend a business. Take inventory of what you are good at and extend out from your skills. Or determine what your customers need and work backwards, even if it requires learning new skills. Kindle is an example of working backward." According to Bezos, by relentlessly focusing on the customer, Amazon has been able to create customer-centric experiences and develop products and services that consistently meet and exceed expectations. Hence, the method has helped Amazon stay at the forefront of e-commerce and expand into various other industries.

Ultimately, the Working Backwards method championed by Jeff Bezos is a customer-centric approach to product development and innovation. By starting with the customer's needs and working backwards, companies can align their efforts and resources to deliver exceptional products and services. This method promotes discipline, creativity, and a culture of experimentation, ultimately leading to increased customer satisfaction and business success. Therefore, the Working Backwards method is one of the most effective ways to achieve success as an entrepreneur.

Lesson: *A customer-centric mindset throughout the development process helps avoid focusing solely on internal aspects or technical details.*

❑

Our Choices Define Us

Our choices have a profound influence on shaping who we are as individuals. They serve as a reflection of our values, beliefs, and priorities, ultimately defining our character and determining the paths we traverse in life. While each choice may seem isolated, the increasing effect of our decisions is what truly defines us.

According to Bezos, every decision we make, whether significant or seemingly trivial, carries consequences that ripple through our lives. Each choice presents an opportunity to express our authentic selves, to align our actions with our principles, and to create the life we desire. It is through the accumulation of these choices that our identity takes shape. Hence, Bezos encourages individuals to take ownership of their choices and embrace the accountability that comes with them.

Recounting his past, in a speech Bezos once said, "I was working at a financial firm in New York city with a bunch of smart people and I had a brilliant boss whom I much admired. I went to my boss and told him that I was going to start a company selling books on the internet. He took me on a long walk-in central park, listened carefully to me and finally said that it sounds like a really good idea but it would be even a better idea for someone who did not already have a decent job." He continued, "Seen in that light, it really was a difficult choice but ultimately, I decided to give it a shot. Today, I am proud of that choice. We all get to choose our life stories and it is our choices that define us."

Bezos believes that we all should be proud of our choices because they reflect who we are and who we want to be in future. We can either choose a life of comfort and ease or life of service and adventure. He further points out that our choices reflect our values and beliefs, acting as a mirror that reveals the essence of who we are. They demonstrate whether we prioritize integrity, kindness, empathy, or ambition. Our decisions in relationships, career, personal growth, and societal engagement demonstrate the core principles that guide us.

Recognizing the power of choices, Bezos advocates individuals to take control of their lives and pursue their aspirations with determination. He encourages people to reflect on the consequences of their decisions and use those insights to fuel personal growth and development. Bezos himself has exemplified this mindset through his entrepreneurial journey, where his bold choices and visionary leadership have propelled Amazon to unprecedented heights.

Furthermore, Bezos stresses how our choices have a cumulative effect, leading us down to particular paths and influencing the opportunities that come our way. The choices we make today shape the options available to us tomorrow. They create a trajectory that becomes intertwined with our identity, impacting our future possibilities and the person we become.

However, Bezos acknowledges that our choices are not made in isolation. They are influenced by our environment, circumstances, and the perspectives of others. Yet, even in the face of external factors, our ability to make conscious choices and taking ownership of our actions remains within our control. It is through these choices that we assert our free will and actively shape our lives.

Therefore, it is essential to remember that our choices are not mere isolated moments; they define us. They reflect our values, shape our experiences, and create our trajectory. Each decision, regardless of its scale, contributes to the accumulation of our character and influences the path we walk. By embracing the power of our choices and acting in alignment with our true selves, we have the opportunity to craft a life that reflects our authentic identity and leaves a lasting and enduring impact on ourselves and those around us.

Lesson: *By aligning our actions with our true selves, we can create a life that leaves a lasting impact.*

❑

Be Intuitive

Being intuitive refers to the ability to make decisions or judgments based on instinct, gut feelings, or a deep-seated understanding without relying solely on explicit reasoning or logical analysis. It involves tapping into one's subconscious knowledge, experience, and pattern recognition to arrive at insights and make informed choices.

Bezos recognized the importance of following one's intuition in decision-making and problem solving. He advocates to combine data-driven analysis with intuition because he understands that while data and analytics provide valuable insights, there are situations where intuitive leaps and gut feelings play a critical role in making successful decisions.

In an interview, Bezos observed, "All my best decisions in business and in life have been made with heart, intuition, guts and not with analysis." Hence, he encourages entrepreneurs and business leaders to cultivate and trust their intuition, especially in confusing or uncertain circumstances. He acknowledges that intuition can help individuals navigate uncharted territories and make decisions with limited information.

According to Bezos, following your gut feeling or intuition can be essential for several reasons. Firstly, in fast-paced business environments, there may not always be enough time to gather extensive data or conduct thorough analysis. Intuition allows business leaders to make quick decisions based on their instincts, drawing upon their wealth of knowledge and experience. Thus, proving itself valuable in time-sensitive situations where delaying a decision might result in missed opportunities.

Secondly, business landscapes often involve uncertainty and ambiguity, especially when exploring new markets, adopting emerging technologies, or venturing into uncharted territories. Intuition can provide guidance and help entrepreneurs navigate through these uncertain waters, as it taps into subtle cues and signals that may not be immediately evident through traditional analysis.

Thirdly, intuition can be a powerful tool for recognizing potential opportunities that may not be easily quantifiable or apparent through data alone. It enables entrepreneurs to spot emerging trends, consumer preferences, or market gaps that others may overlook. Following one's gut feeling can lead to the discovery of unique business prospects and competitive advantages.

Furthermore, Bezos points out and affirms that intuition often plays an important role in fostering creative thinking and innovative solutions. Being intuitive allows business leaders to connect seemingly unrelated ideas or concepts, leading to breakthrough innovations. By trusting their intuition, entrepreneurs can challenge conventional thinking and take calculated risks that lead to disruptive ideas and competitive differentiation.

Finally, intuition can be instrumental in building meaningful relationships and understanding the needs and desires of customers, employees, and partners. By listening to their instincts, business leaders can empathize with others, anticipate their motivations, and make decisions that resonate with their target audience. This emotional intelligence can contribute to stronger rapport, trust, and loyalty.

However, Bezos suggests that intuition should not be solely relied upon in isolation. It should be complemented by a solid foundation of data-driven analysis, market research, and critical thinking. Combining intuition with rational decision-making processes can enhance overall business acumen and increase the likelihood of success.

As Bezos often says, "If you can make a decision with analysis, you should do so. But it turns out that in life your most important decisions are always made with instinct and intuition, taste, heart." Therefore, trust your instincts when making life's most important decisions, and then put in concerted efforts to prove it right. Remember your true wisdom manifests in the subconscious. So, trust your intuition.

Lesson: *Intuition is valuable in time-sensitive environments where extensive data may not be available. It helps navigate ambiguity and uncover potential opportunities that may be overlooked.*

❑

Start Working as Early as Possible

During his time in high school, Jeff Bezos worked at McDonald's as a short-order line cook during the breakfast shift. This experience taught him valuable lessons that extended beyond earning some extra cash. Working at a young age provides numerous benefits, including learning about money management, developing interpersonal skills, and cultivating a strong work ethic. These lessons have an enduring impact on financial success in adulthood.

Bezos believes that by working at an early age, teenagers gain firsthand experience in handling money and understanding its value. Earning an early pay cheque teaches them the importance of budgeting, making wise financial decisions, and developing a saving habit. This early exposure to financial responsibility sets a strong foundation for their future financial well-being.

Bezos also acknowledges that early work experiences provide an opportunity to develop essential work skills and gain practical knowledge. By entering the workforce early, individuals can learn about professionalism, time management, teamwork, and problem-solving. These skills are indispensable and become valuable assets throughout their careers.

Furthermore, Bezos recommends to start working early because it provides individuals a platform for networking and building social skills. Young individuals have the opportunity to interact with diverse groups of people, develop professional relationships, and expand their professional networks. These connections can be proved valuable for future career opportunities and personal growth.

On top of that, Bezos suggest that early work experiences enable individuals to make informed decisions about their future. By gaining exposure to different industries and job roles, young individuals can refine their career aspirations and make more informed choices regarding their education and professional path. It helps them align their academic pursuits with their long-term goals and objectives.

Ultimately, Bezos feels that having early work experience enhances employability in the future. Employers often value candidates who have a track record of early work experiences, as it demonstrates initiative, a strong work ethic, and the ability to handle responsibilities. It provides a competitive edge when applying for internships, scholarships, or future employment opportunities.

Bezos recognize that as adults, it is important to encourage young people, including our own children, to start working at an early age. This experience helps them grasp the importance of money, develop a sense of financial responsibility, and instil effective money management habits. It also teaches them the significance of having a budget, saving for the future, and cultivating positive relationships with colleagues and customers.

However, it is crucial for young individuals to perceive work not as a punishment, but as an opportunity for personal growth and learning. By understanding the value of work from an early age, they gain a sense of responsibility, discipline, and independence. This mindset sets them on a path towards financial stability and success in their adult lives.

Therefore, start working in life as early as possible because it teaches individuals the value of money, imparts essential skills in human relationships and work ethics, and sets them on a path towards financial success in adulthood.

Lesson: *Work at an early age to gain firsthand experience with money, budgeting, and savings. Early work experiences also provide essential skills like professionalism.*

❑

Learn Humility

In the vast landscape of entrepreneurial triumphs and corporate conquests, one aspect often overlooked, yet paramount, is humility. Bezos has noticed that the most intelligent individuals are consistently modifying their understanding by reassessing problems they believed they had already resolved. They exhibit openness to fresh perspectives, new data, innovative concepts, inconsistencies, and challenges to their established thought processes.

According to Bezos, to reach your maximum potential, you need to be willing to learn and improve. And that necessarily entails admitting you do not already have all the answers. That is why, at the core of Bezos's perspective lies the understanding that humility serves as the cornerstone for continuous learning and growth. It is the humble acknowledgement of one's limitations and the openness to new ideas that enable individuals to evolve and adapt in an ever-evolving business landscape.

In Bezos's opinion, great leaders are those who understand that they are not the smartest person in the room. Nor do they have to be. Instead, they encourage individuals to express themselves, respect different perspectives and support great ideas, regardless of their origin. In fact, Bezos has observed that the smartest people are constantly revising their understanding, reconsidering a problem they thought they had already solved. They are open to new points of view, new information, new ideas, contradictions, and challenges to their own way of thinking.

Moreover, Bezos points out that humility helps to foster positive relationships. It is observed that individuals who are humble in nature are more approachable than those people who are egoistical in nature. It is important to note that being humble does not mean thinking less of yourself but it means to realize that there are many individuals who are more knowledgeable or successful then them.

Therefore, remember that humility is not a sign of weakness but rather a strength that enhances personal development, enriches relationships, and contributes to the creation of a more compassionate and collaborative world.

In an interview, Bezos has mentioned that while hiring professionals he often looks for people who have a few failures under the belt. The reason behind his actions is not to hire risk-takers but to hire individuals who are smart and confident enough to admit when they are wrong and search for better ideas.

In fact, there are instances where Bezos has emphasized the importance of staying humble and being open to learning. For example, in Amazon's early days, Bezos worked alongside his employees in the company's distribution centres during peak seasons. This hands-on approach demonstrated his willingness to engage in the day-to-day operations of the business and to understand the challenges faced by his employees.

Additionally, Bezos has acknowledged the role of failure in the process of innovation. His perspective on failure reflects a humble acknowledgement that not every endeavour will be successful, and that learning from failures is an integral part of achieving long-term success.

This is why, it is important to always be humble in nature despite of how successful you are because it is not necessary that you will be at your best. There will be times when you will be wrong and fail in your endeavours. So, learn to be humble in all scenarios, and appreciate and value the contribution of others.

Lesson: *Great leaders understand that they are not the smartest person in the room, encouraging diverse opinions and supporting innovative ideas. Humility also fosters positive relationships, making individuals more approachable.*

❑